AL SARRANTONIO

COLD NIGHT

TOR

A TOM DOHERTY ASSOCIATES BOOK
NEW YORK

This is a work of fiction. All the characters and events portrayed in this book are fictitious, and any resemblance to real people or events is purely coincidental.

COLD NIGHT

A TOR BOOK

Published by Tom Doherty Associates, Inc.
49 West 24 Street
New York, NY 10010

Sarrantonio, Al.
  Cold night / Al Sarrantonio.—1st ed.
  "A Tom Doherty Associates book."
  ISBN 0-312-93147-6
  I. Title.
PS3569.A73C65   1989
813'.54—dc19   88-29169

First edition: March 1989
0 9 8 7 6 5 4 3 2 1

For
Joanne Martin and Mary Ellen Kovalchik
Two of the Good Ones

There is the heat of day,
And then there is cold night.

—Otto Stiegler

O·N·E

Someone on the other end of the phone said, "Barker Agency?"

"Yes."

"Who's this?"

"Paine."

"You'll do. I want you to go to the Mallard Hotel and ask at the desk for a letter addressed to Mr. Johnson from Mr. Grumbach. I'm Grumbach. You'll be Johnson. The letter will tell you what has to be done. There are five one-hundred-dollar bills in the envelope along with the letter. That's your payment. There won't be anything but a verbal contract on this, but I'm assuming I can trust you to do what the letter says."

"My boss won't let me work without a written contract," Paine said.

"You'll have to," Grumbach said.

"Why?"

"I'm going to hang myself."

"Mr. Grumbach?" Paine said, but then he heard what sounded like the tap of a phone being laid on a table and then the scrape and fall of a chair. He heard a single strangled cry, and then a terrible gasping, and then he heard what he imagined to be the man's feet kicking the phone from its table. He heard the loud bang of a phone receiver hitting the floor, and then silence.

"Mr. Grumbach?" Paine said evenly into the phone.

There was no answer.

Paine's hand was trembling.

"Oh, Jesus," he said.

T·W·O

The front lawn was a golf course without holes in it. Paine stepped out of his car and across the driveway onto the lawn until a scowl from the gardener working in a picture-perfect rock garden with miniature roses and tulips made him hop off it onto a flagstone path.

The bell rang once, deep inside the house. The door opened almost immediately, showing an expanse of marble floor as long and nearly as wide as the front lawn. There seemed to be no one holding the door, but when Paine walked in, a maid stepped from behind the door in front of him, blocking his way.

"To the left," she said, making it clear that the rest of the house was not anywhere he was allowed to go.

He went into a room with nothing in it a lighter shade than dark green. The wooden shutters were closed, but the little bars of light that got in from the brilliant sun outside showed him a typical man's room: trophies, a television three feet diagonal or so, a leather-padded bar, leather chairs. He was peering closely in the dim light at one of the rifles mounted on the wall, a .30-06, when an amber light went on behind him, pushing the room into twilight, and the girl who had agreed to see him walked in.

"We're all good shots in this family," she said to the rifle, and then she said to Paine, "I'm Dolores Grumbach."

He saw that he was supposed to cross the room to meet her at the door, so he stayed where he was. Something flashed across her eyes for a moment, something that made the room almost bright, but then it disappeared and a trace of smile came onto her face. She was all of nineteen, Paine thought, but the smile was a tired one.

"You have something to show me?" she said. "You said on the phone you had something from my father. If you don't mind I'd like you to give it to me and leave."

Paine said nothing.

She looked at him for a moment, and then she turned toward the bar and pulled a glass from a long neat line of them. Paine saw that her hand was shaking, ever so slightly. With practiced ease she uncapped a decanter and poured just enough whiskey into the glass to make the ice she added sparkle with the same amber color as the room.

"Would you like a drink, Mr. Paine?" she said, not turning around.

"No," Paine said.

"Can I make you one, anyway?"

"If you like."

She repeated the smooth motions with the glass, liquor and ice and then she turned to him, waiting again for him to come to her. This time he did, reaching out to take the glass. Her fingers touched his hand, and they were as cold and wet as the glass. Her nails were short and uneven. She left the glass in his hand and lowered herself onto one of the padded barstools.

"To you, Mr. Paine," she said mirthlessly, and she downed the whiskey in a smooth motion.

Paine held the glass in his hand. He felt the ice melt inside it. A long minute passed. Dolores Grumbach did not look at him. Finally, she put the glass down on the bar, the violence of the motion dulled by the leather padding.

"Did you see him before anyone else did?" she asked.

"No. I called the police and let them do that. I went up with them, but I didn't go in first and when I did go in, there was nothing for me to see. He didn't leave a note in the room. There was nothing on him but his wallet."

"Was it an awful place?"

"Yes, it was," Paine said. "A garbage hotel. He had a room with a single bulb in it, with no washstand, no blanket on the bed, dirty floor, water marks on the walls. It smelled bad."

"We buried him this morning." She stared somewhere far off.

"Miss Grumbach," Paine said, "I don't think your father killed himself."

She came back from where she had been. "Tell me what you mean," she said. Her eyes were flat brown in her face.

"What do *you* think about it?" Paine asked.

"I think," she said, "that he killed himself."

"Why?"

She laughed hollowly. "Because that's what I choose to believe."

Paine looked at her, but she said nothing.

"What is it you wanted?" she asked him.

Paine reached into his pocket and brought out an envelope. The name "Mr. Johnson" was scribbled across the front. He handed it to her.

"Is that your father's handwriting?"

"It is," she said.

"Are you sure?"

Her eyes didn't look at the envelope again.

"Yes."

"Look inside."

She slipped her hand into the envelope and brought out five new one-hundred-dollar bills and three black-and-white glossy photographs. She put the hundred-dollar bills on the bar behind her, not looking at them, and then she looked at the photographs casually, one after the other. They were copy prints of old photos: two showed a couple each, a smiling man and woman next to a new car and in the other an older man and woman, she smiling slightly, the man frowning. There was what looked like a horse in the background, and a fuzzy field bordered by eucalyptus trees sloping up to the horizon. The third photo was of a man only, in a suit and tie; it looked like the kind of thing corporations put in their newsletters when someone gets promoted, the head turned slightly to one side, face set, mouth in a half-serious smile.

She finished with the photographs and put them back in the envelope and handed the envelope to Paine.

"Who are they?" she asked him.

"I thought you might tell me that."

"I don't think I want to."

"Would you look at them again? Closely this time."

"I saw them," she said. "I don't want to know any of those people."

"All right," Paine said, half to himself. The girl was refilling her glass.

"Want another drink?" she asked.

"No," he said, looking at the untouched one in his hand.

She sat facing the bar, away from him.

"Miss Grumbach," he said, "your father hired me, over the phone, just before he died. He told me my instructions would be inside the envelope you're holding, and that I would find it under the name 'Johnson' at the Mallard Hotel. There's no note in there, only those photographs. The truth is, I'm not allowed to work for anyone without a written, signed contract between the client and the Barker Agency, for whom I work. Your father died before he signed that contract. Now the only way I can continue with this is if someone else—"

"I'll think about it," she said from her faraway place. She took the five hundred-dollar bills from the bar and slid them back into the envelope, handing it back to him. "I assume this money was to be your payment. Keep it. Give me your contract if you want."

Paine gave her the folded contract from his inside jacket pocket. He saw that her glass was empty. She rose from the barstool, steadily, and began to walk to the doorway.

"Find out whatever you want," she said.

"You told me he killed himself."

"I said that's what I wanted to think," she said. "We all want a lot of things, Mr. Paine."

"I'll need—"

"I'll think about it. I'm tired. I'm going to bathe."

She left the room. She turned out the amber light, and Paine was left in semidarkness. Though it was dark and cool in the room he could sense the heat outside; the thin slats of light that fell into the room were bright against the leather chairs they settled on. He put the envelope back into his pocket and made his way to the door.

As he stepped out, there were voices in the hallway. Approaching him was a fuller, healthier, slightly older version of Dolores Grumbach. She wore tennis shorts, and her hair was cut boyishly short. Paine saw a man, short-haired, healthy-looking, dressed also in tennis whites, mounting the marble steps at the end of the hallway.

"You must be Mr. Paine?" the woman said. She held out a long slim hand. "I'm Dolores's sister, Rebecca Meyer."

Paine took her hand; she curled her fingers around his, holding them an instant too long.

"I hope you didn't find my sister too full of ennui," she said, smiling slightly. "Part of it's an act."

"Part?" Paine said.

She kept her eyes on him, and then they suddenly wrinkled up at the corners and she asked, smiling, "Would you like a drink?"

"I was already offered one, thanks," he said. He took out the envelope again, removing the three photographs. "Would you mind telling me if you know any of these people?"

She took the photographs from him and concentrated on each one. She shook her head. "I'm sorry, no." She handed them back. "Won't you please have that drink?"

She put a hand on his arm and Paine felt a tingle where her fingers rested.

Paine put the photos away.

"I really have to go."

"Maybe next time, then."

"Maybe next time."

He went to the front door and the maid was there, holding it open. Then suddenly he was outside, in the bright sun, feeling the gardener's eyes keeping him on the flagstone walk until he got to his car.

T·H·R·E·E

Jimmy Carnaseca was building something on his desk.

"What the hell is that?" Paine asked.

Jimmy kept his eyes on the thing on his desk, but his mouth turned up into a delighted grin. "Something I picked up on the way in." He was fitting tiny sticks together, little bigger than toothpicks, perfectly slotted on each end so that they fit together without falling apart. It crowded out half the desktop; the telephone had been moved and there were papers restacked on one side, in a rough pile away from the construction.

"Looks like a bridge," Paine said, sitting down in the desk chair and swiveling it away from Jimmy.

"Something like that. You'll see when it's done."

"Barker in?"

Jimmy frowned. "Not yet."

"Good."

"You'd better watch out," Jimmy said. "He'll chew your ass off, spit it out the window."

"He wouldn't know where to chew."

Jimmy continued with his tinkering, until Paine asked, "Coffee boy been by yet?"

"No."

"That's good, too."

"What's eating you?" Jimmy said, stopping his work. He stood as straight as his small, bent frame would let him. He stared unblinking at Paine, a tiny wooden girder held delicately in his fingers.

"You should have been a surgeon, Jimmy," Paine said.

Jimmy said, "I asked you what's eating you."

"Nothing much. Coffee boy been by yet?"

Jimmy stared at him.

"Sorry, Jimmy," Paine said.

Carnaseca regarded him dispassionately for a moment. "What is it, Jack?"

Paine said nothing. Then he said, "Lots of things, Jimmy."

"Love trouble?"

Paine looked at him. "I suppose that's part of it."

"You should do like I do," Carnaseca said. He began to work again, humming to himself.

"And what do you do?" Paine found himself smiling.

Jimmy kept humming. He shook his head, a grin splitting his face.

"I ought to knock this thing down . . ." Paine threatened, holding his fist playfully over Carnaseca's model.

"Bastard," Jimmy said.

There was a banging out in the hallway. Paine cursed.

"Speaking of bastards," he said.

He wheeled the chair away from the doorway as someone large walked past. There came a loud noise at the other end of the hall, a door opening and then slamming shut. They heard papers being scattered about, and then another figure, a thin, pretty woman, hurried by with a stack of papers in her hands. She moved with an odd limp. A moment later they heard the door at the end of the hall squeaking open and then shutting again.

A voice roared, words not discernible.

"Shitbag," Paine said.

"I think I heard the coffee boy," Jimmy said, laying the sticks of wood in his hand down and putting all the strays into a box which he carefully closed, hiding the cover under a stack of papers. He pointed to the wooden construction. "Don't mess that up, you louse. Want anything?"

"No," Paine said.

Paine got up and went to his own office. He didn't want to open the door; he wanted to go back to Jimmy's chair and sit where there was light and books on the walls and a little sun coming through. Jimmy even had a personal file; it was in the middle drawer of his file cabinet in a blue hanging folder. "Anything ever happens to me," Jimmy had told him once, grinning, "it's all there. You can read it if you want." Paine had no personal file in his office. It was all in his head, and he didn't want anyone to read it. He didn't want to read it himself. He felt a cold draft through the darkened glass pane of the door that didn't have his name stenciled on it.

He turned the knob and went in.

The light went on, but it was as dark in the room as it had been in Morris Grumbach's study. *A tomb,* Paine thought. He almost felt a touch on his hand as he released the light switch but it was only a movement of cold air over his knuckles, from the ventilator duct overhead.

The telephone was a black glossy shape on a gray-topped, empty desk that didn't even have a blotter on it. The chair was tilted back at an unnatural angle, the padding torn through, part of it pulled out. Jimmy had told him that Barker had deliberately taken that chair out of storage and put it in his room so that he would have to sit on it.

He sat on the edge of the desk, taking in the stacks of files on top of overstuffed cabinets; the venetian blinds jammed in a closed position, a quarter inch of dust settled like dirty snow across the strips of white aluminum; the fan overhead that didn't work; the cracks in the ceiling, some of which led down the walls to hit the floor in a spread of tributaries.

Nice life you've got here, Paine thought.

A tomb.

His hand dangled over the phone, fell on it, turned the receiver aside and started to dial a number. His hand stopped, put the receiver down and then picked it up again, with more determination.

"Jack?" someone asked quietly from the door, knocking politely and then opening it.

The phone fell back into the cradle.

"What is it, Margie?" Paine asked.

"He wants to see you."

She wore her perpetual hurt look. Paine had noticed her limp before, but now he saw that she wore a baggy kind of dress that fell nearly to the floor. Jimmy had told him what her legs looked like under that dress, how smooth and white one of them was, how twisted and mangled the other was.

"What does he want, Margie?"

Her pinched look stayed.

"All right," Paine said.

He pulled himself off the desk. As he stepped into the hallway Jimmy Carneseca was there, pressing the Velcro tab down on his camera bag. He had a Styrofoam cup of coffee in his other hand, a spurt of steam rising from a corner where the plastic lid was pried up. "Got to catch somebody cheating on somebody," he grinned, moving past. "Don't let anybody mess with that thing on my desk."

"Sure, Jimmy."

Paine was alone in the hallway. He looked at the wall and suddenly it was moving at him, looking to squeeze him back until he was caught. Then it would come at him, pushing, pushing, until all the air was gone—

A tomb.

He closed his eyes tight and gently moved the panic away from his mind. In a moment, he was breathing easily. His hands unclenched. They were cold, covered with sweat. His forehead was covered with sweat, too. He took a deep breath and looked at the far wall. It was only a wall again, made white-yellow by the lights overhead.

Okay, Jack, he thought. *Okay.*

He walked into Barker's office.

There was stenciled lettering a half-foot high on the door. It said "Robert Barker," in script. Inside, Barker was yelling, but the yelling abruptly stopped. The door opened and Margie hurried out, dipping under Paine's arm.

"Go on," she said.

Barker was in his chair with his back to him, facing the window. Jimmy had explained that the room was set up strategically. Barker faced away from you; you walked around the desk and the audience began when you were standing with your back to the window. You sat down in a low chair and Barker looked down at you. He was not as big as he looked. His suits were cut a little large, the shoulders padded; he had had his head shaved to look older and tougher. His shoes had heels laid a little higher than normal. He wore thick glasses though there was nothing wrong with his eyes. He was manicured and tailored to perfection, the knot in his tie so sharp you could cut yourself on it. He favored a large ring on his right pinky, a round sapphire surrounded by brilliant diamond chips. He kept the nails on his fingers longer than they should be. He was an illusion, but the illusion worked.

"You wanted me," Paine said from the doorway, to Barker's back.

"I don't want you," Barker said from behind his chair. "I sent for you."

A thin plume of ochre smoke rose from Barker's Dunhill cigarette, and finally Paine went all the way in.

He walked past the dark green plants, perfectly kept by Margie; the bookcases with leather volumes that had never been touched, the cases jutting out far into the room to make it seem claustrophobic on the visitor's side though in fact the place was huge. Music played softly through hidden speakers—Rachmaninoff, a piano sparring with a full orchestra, strangely muted by the lowness of the volume. A chair was left in the pathway, deliberately, so that the visitor had to step around it, coming close to Barker's high-backed lounge chair and desk but not touching it.

Paine negotiated these obstacles and stood finally on the other side of the desk, in the light from the window.

"What do you want?" Paine said, standing.

"Sit," Barker said.

Paine sat down in the low chair, and Barker loomed judiciously in front of him.

"How many cases do you have at the moment?" Barker said.

"Just this Grumbach business."

"Just what is it you do around here?" Barker inquired mildly. His hand was cocked at an angle, holding his thin cigarette so that the smoke went up at just the right angle away from his face, as if he was posing.

"What is it you wanted?" Paine answered.

"Didn't you hear my question?" Barker said. "I asked: Just what is it you do around here?"

"I work for you," Paine replied evenly. "I work in your freak show."

Barker leaned back into the softness of the chair and put his cigarette into his mouth. He drew on it slowly, said nothing.

"How old are you?" he asked finally.

Paine sighed. "Thirty-six."

"How long would you have been on the police force if you weren't here now?"

Despite rising anger, Paine began to count years in his head.

Barker answered for him: "Fourteen years. Six more and you would have been up for retirement. Here's another question. What would you be doing if you were not working for me?"

Paine was silent.

"Come on now," Barker said, waving his cigarette in front of him. "Give me an answer."

"I'd be cleaning your toilets."

A moment went by, and then Barker began to laugh. The cultivated titter he usually affected was overcome by great bursts of throaty noise. It was the kind of laughter a rude man in an audience makes when a juggler drops one of his tenpins. Barker leaned forward, his hand on his chest; he was wheezing with laughter. He put his delicate hands on the desk before him to steady himself. Eventually, his face relaxed.

"Thank you," he said, leaning back, "for saying what I'd hoped you would."

Paine started to get up.

"Sit down, Paine," Barker said.

Despite his anger, Paine released the handrests and sat back down.

"I don't like you at all," Barker said. "In many ways, you're the biggest loser I've ever taken on. A failed police career, failing marriage, in and out of alcohol treatment centers and psychological counseling." Barker held up a manicured finger, searching for the phrase he wanted. "And yet here you are, working for me, because no one else will have you. Isn't that marvelous?"

Paine said, "I don't like it much, either."

Barker smiled, threatening to break into his laugh again. "Paine, I couldn't care less if you like me or not. To me you're just another of my—"

"Cripples?" There was something hot inside Paine that wanted to boil out. But that was what Barker wanted. With effort Paine let the moment of heat pass.

"Perhaps one day you'll clean my toilets," Barker said, swiveling his chair toward the invisible speakers that were now bringing the Rachmaninoff Third Piano Concerto to a muted halt, "but now you do other things for me. While you were playing with Jimmy Carnaseca I took a telephone call of yours, from a Ms."—he looked down at a slip of paper in front of him—"Meyer. One of Grumbach's daughters, as you *should* already know. Her younger sister spoke with you at length this morning about signing one of our contracts." Barker didn't look up, but creased the slip of memo paper between his fingers. "Ms. Meyer said she has the signed contract for you, and that her sister left instructions that you stop by the Mallard Hotel." He swiveled completely away from Paine. The hidden stereo, its tape rewound, once again started on the Rachmaninoff piece. "She said her sister committed suicide this morning."

F·O·U·R

Y ou have a letter for Mr. Paine?"
The lobby of the Mallard Hotel was crowded,
but the desk clerk recognized him, anyway.

"Aren't you Mr. Johnson?"

"My name is Paine." He showed the clerk his driver's
license and a credit card.

The clerk was gone a minute, then returned empty-
handed.

"Sorry, nothing for Mr. Paine. But there's another letter
for Mr. Johnson."

"I'll take it."

"But you said—"

"Now I'm Mr. Johnson. Get the letter."

He held a five-dollar bill out on the end of his fingers like
a Christmas ornament. The clerk returned with an envelope. He hesitated before taking the money.

"The Mallard is a good hotel, Mr. Paine."

"And I'm a good customer," Paine said, taking the envelope firmly from him and dropping the five-dollar bill on the desk.

When he got to his car he opened the envelope and drew out three photographs. There was nothing else. He spread the photos out on the seat. They were not the same as the others. These were three head shots of three different men. All of them looked like car salesmen. They looked like three salesmen for the same Plymouth dealership.

Paine put the photos back into the envelope, holding it in his hand for a moment before putting it into his jacket pocket and starting the car.

This time the Grumbach estate was alive with activity. There were two police cars parked at an angle in the circular drive, two vans with leading cables that could only be television crews. Two suicides in the same moneyed family in one week was obviously news. The gardener was nowhere to be seen. At the front door Paine waited for the ghostly maid to answer, but the door was opened by Rebecca Meyer.

She was again in tennis whites. But now there were red puffy patches under her eyes, and her short hair was in disarray. As Paine stood there she brought her fingers up to her hair and drew them through it, making a nervous motion with her other hand.

"Come in," she said.

Paine took a step but she suddenly held her hand out and added, "No, don't. Let's walk." She stepped out quickly, closing the door behind her.

"I hope you don't mind," she said as she brought him around the front of the house, across the manicured miniature garden and onto a flat-stoned path toward the side. "I just can't stand it in there. The television people, the police, it's . . . ghoulish." Once again her hand made its way up to her hair, but this time a tremble ran down her arm and made her shiver. "I'm sorry."

Paine said nothing, because she wanted to talk.

"My father," she said, "I was not very close to. In all honesty, I can say that when he killed himself I . . . wasn't very sorry about it. But Dolores . . ." The name trailed off; her hand made a movement out in front of her.

She regained some of her poise. They had rounded the side of the house and were making their way through a copse of trees as pampered as the rest of the grounds; each branch seemed sculpted to fit with every other, and there was not a leaf or blade of grass out of place.

Rebecca Meyer said, "I suppose that must sound hard, or something, my not feeling anything for my father?"

When Paine said nothing she added, "You think I'm cruel."

"I don't know you," Paine said.

"That's true," she said. "But I wanted you to know that . . . I was not very close to my parents."

"Not many people are."

"Dolores and I got along better when we were younger. She's been a troubled girl the past few years."

"Lots of people are troubled."

"You're mocking me."

"No, I'm not," Paine said.

Rebecca Meyer stopped for a moment. She looked like she was going to cry. "I found her. She'd locked the bathroom door. She'd taken a bottle of sleeping pills and run a hot bath. She was dead when they got her to the hospital."

Paine thought of Dolores Grumbach drinking in front of him, telling him she was going to take a bath, just before he left her.

"Did she leave a note for you, or anyone else?"

"Just that note for you, laid neatly on top of the signed contract for your agency." She pulled a creased set of papers from the pocket of her windbreaker and handed it to Paine.

"Mr. Paine," the note read, "there is something for you at the Mallard Hotel. Enclosed are the signed contracts you requested. Give one copy to my sister Rebecca. The check attached will cover any initial expenses my father's money does not; I am sure my sister will give you whatever else you need." It was signed in neat script, "Dolores Grumbach."

There was a check for five hundred dollars clipped to the contracts. Paine looked up at Rebecca Meyer. She was regarding him curiously, her eyes searching his face.

"This is all there was?" Paine asked.

"Yes. Will you tell me what my sister left for you at the Mallard Hotel?"

Paine handed the three new photographs to Rebecca Meyer. She turned through them slowly, more carefully than she had when looking over the first set of black-and-whites.

"Have you ever seen any of them before?"

"Yes." She pointed to one photo of a man with short sideburns and a pin-striped suit. "This is Les Paterna," she said. "He worked with my father for a while, about ten years ago."

"Can you tell me anything about him? Was he close to the family?"

"He was at the house occasionally."

Paine put the photographs away. "Do you know where I might be able to reach him?"

"He's in the Westchester phone book. His company is called Bravura Enterprises."

They had reached the end of the path. It opened onto a vast glide of lawn. To the right, at the bottom of a hill, a flat tennis court was bounded by green fencing; behind that were a swimming pool and a skeet shooting range. To the left the lawn kept going, rising and falling steadily downward, till the Hudson River, a sparkling blue hedge of water, cut the world in two.

They moved gradually down to the right, stopping by the green chain link surrounding the tennis court. There was a bench, the kind you order from a store in Vermont, with strong pine planking laid across a green wrought-iron frame. Rebecca Meyer sat down. On the tennis court someone had left a towel and a pair of sunglasses. A racket had been tossed carelessly aside to land on the white foul line.

"I didn't tell the police about you or the note," Rebecca Meyer said.

"That will help."

"It's not any of their business."

Paine found himself drawn to look into her eyes, which were studying him again. There was something about her that he couldn't put his finger on. Something that disturbed and attracted him.

"I find it easy to talk to you," Rebecca Meyer said. The slightest of smiles touched her lips as she put her hand on his. "Would you mind telling me why?"

Paine drew his hand politely away from hers and put it on his lap.

After a moment, he asked her, "How close were you to your sister?"

"I loved Dolores very much. But I can't say we were very close. She was moody and cynical. When she was in school she spent most of her time by herself. She read a lot. My mother doted on her as much as on any of us, but all I can remember Dolores asking Mother for were books. My sister Gloria and I watched television and played tennis, Dolores read books."

They looked at the chain link fence.

"Is your sister Gloria here?" Paine asked.

"She was down from Boston for my father's funeral yesterday and then went home to her family. She'll be back tonight."

"Was she very close to Dolores?"

"Gloria is close to no one."

"Not even to your mother?"

Rebecca nearly laughed. "Gloria is exactly like my mother."

Paine waited for her to say more.

"My sister Gloria," she went on, "is gracious, smooth, cold, and everyone loves her." She stopped, took a long breath. "I'm sorry if that sounds bitter, but it's true. My mother and she always got what they wanted, which was everything."

"Your mother—"

"She died a year ago," Rebecca Meyer said. Then she added abruptly, "I think we should be getting back."

She got up and Paine went with her back toward the house. As they reached the grove of trees, Paine saw the man he had seen the day before. He was out of his tennis outfit today, leaning in a polo shirt and chinos against a tree bordering the path.

"The police have been looking for you," he said to Rebecca.

She brushed past him. "I told them all there was. This is Mr. Paine, a detective. This is Gerald."

"I know," Gerald said. "I told Inspector Dannon that Paine was here."

Rebecca turned on him. "I told you we were going to keep him out of this," she said between her teeth.

He spread his hands innocently. "What could I do? They asked where you were."

"Idiot," she said, continuing on to the house with Paine.

"I'd better go," Paine said.

She took his arm, squeezing. "Please," she said. "Not yet."

Dannon was waiting for them in the front driveway by the open door to his car. The TV crews had vanished, looking for other carrion.

"Mrs. Meyer," Dannon said politely, "there was just one other thing I wanted to ask you. Your husband mentioned something about a note your sister left." He didn't look at Paine.

Paine took the note from his pocket and handed it to Dannon. "It was a business matter between her and me. Not a suicide note, if that makes you feel better."

Dannon ignored Paine and took the note. He read it over quickly, then brought his eyes level with Paine's. "Mrs. Meyer's husband said something about some other papers, too." He pointed at the note. "What's this about something for you at the Mallard Hotel?"

Paine handed Dannon the agency contracts and the check. "The Mallard Hotel thing didn't exist," he said evenly. "They had nothing for me there. Look into it if you want."

"Are you fucking with me?" Dannon spat. Immediately he turned to Rebecca Meyer to apologize.

"No," Paine said. "Check it if you want. Ask the afternoon clerk if there was anything for a shithead named Paine."

"Don't fuck with me."

"Farthest thing from my mind."

Dannon's ears turned red, and he put out his balled fists, but Rebecca Meyer intervened.

"Please, Inspector," she said, "Mr. Paine told you the truth." She glanced toward the open door of the car. "Is there anything else you wanted?"

"I guess not."

Paine said, "Let me have that note back."

"No way." Dannon got quickly into his car and closed the door.

He gunned the accelerator and slipped the car into gear. Suddenly he reached out through the open window and grabbed Paine by the arm.

"Don't fuck with me," he whispered. His eyes were tight and hard, and he released the brake, making Paine stumble a few steps along with the car before giving his arm back to him. The car slammed ahead, squealing around the circular driveway, and then was gone through the gates.

Paine stood rubbing his arm as Rebecca Meyer came up to him.

"I had some trouble with that guy once," he explained, his eyes on the gates, the place where the car no longer was.

F·I·V·E

Paine was in one of the bad places.

It wasn't bad to begin with, but it would get bad very soon. He was back with his father, after the long dark space that he didn't want to think about, and his brother, Tom, was there, too. They were all in the house together, just like they had always been, and though it didn't feel the same, though that dark place was just behind him, he knew that this was as close to good as it would ever get again. His father was smiling. They sat around the nicked-up kitchen table and his father made them waffles like he always had on Saturdays. This wasn't Saturday, it was Friday, but that didn't matter because only the waffles mattered. He had slept in his own bed the night before, and he had slept well though there were times during the night when he had come awake clutching the mattress right through the covers, and breathing hard. He had rubbed his wrists, feeling not manacles but only their receding, sore marks. That had happened three or four times, but by late into the night, when it was almost morning, his body had finally realized where it was and he had slept. He must have gotten the good sleep because when he woke he felt as if he had been out for two days. And then he had smelled waffles, and coffee and bacon.

His father served it up on the big plates their mother had bought on sale, the ones that had lasted for years and never got chipped or cracked, even when he or Tom dropped them while washing and cleaning. The coffee smelled good. He saw that his father had put a coffee cup in front of his own plate for him. That had never happened before. Tom was looking at him strangely, but he was smiling, and the strangeness was there only because he was younger and didn't know what was happening.

"Can I have coffee, too, Pop?" Tom asked his father.

"Just sit and shut it," the old man said, but he was smiling even though his hands shook a little on the bacon skillet.

"Damn!" he suddenly blurted out as the skillet tipped back and a dip of bacon grease caught him on the knuckles. Reflexively, he dropped the skillet, and half the bacon slid off to land sizzling on top of the stove. *"Goddamn!"* he said, holding his hand to his side and at the same time trying to fork the bacon slices back onto the pan. "Got to keep your mind on what you're doing all the time," he said, and then he finally had all the bacon back in place, the heat turned down, and he ran some cold water over his hand and swore once more, though softer.

"Hope you boys are hungry," he said, though he didn't look at Tom. He was looking at Jack. "You hungry?" Pop asked again. Jack nodded, and something passed between them. What it was he didn't know, but suddenly he was afraid again, as he hadn't been since he had come home.

But then they were eating waffles, and bacon saved from the ruins of the grease, and he was drinking coffee with his old man and he was happy. He was wearing one of his clean shirts, from his own bureau, and a pair of clean chinos, and his Sunday shoes, and his father was bending over his plate and putting more on it as soon as it was empty.

"Must be hungry," his father said, and he even filled his coffee cup again when it was empty, though the strong-tasting stuff had gone down hard.

"Hurry up now," Pop said, "we got to leave soon."

"Where to?" Tom asked, but Pop turned to him and said, "Not you. You stay here and clean your brother's room. Me and him's got to go out."

Once more, fear took hold of him, but his father reached his big hand over and put it on top of his own and he said softly, "Don't you ever worry again." He took his hand away, suddenly self-conscious, and there was that slight tremble in it again and he got up from the table.

"I'll get the coats," he said.

They went out into the sunshine, and the day was warm and the trees smelled like they should when spring is coming. There were still patches of March snow in the corners, out away from the sun, but the sun was getting high and by the end of the day all the snow would disappear. By the smell of the world they would see no more snow this year. He had never smelled spring like this before, and suddenly it was all through him, in his arms and legs, and he turned to his father.

"Can we go to a ball game soon, Pop?"

His father looked down, from far away. He looked through him for a moment, and then he heard. His mouth smiled and then he laughed.

"Sure. How 'bout opening day at Yankee Stadium?"

"Could we?"

"You bet." And then his father held his hand, very tight, and opened the car door for him and closed it after him.

They drove through the new spring, with the windows down, and then they came to a place that looked familiar, but not the same. He knew he had seen it before, but he knew that this wasn't the way he had seen it; it looked similar, and yet it was different. Nothing was where it was supposed to be, the doors, the windows, but they were the same kinds of doors and windows and the brick was the same color and there was the same kind of green moss between the cracks in the bricks. They parked the car and there was a long ramp leading down, and his father smiled and they walked down it and opened a swinging door and went in.

It was bright inside, and there were people and there was noise. He saw a few men with cameras and large coats. His father pushed his head gently down and made him walk through. His father kept his head down, too. He started to protest but his father hushed him and soon the men and some of the noise were behind them.

"Stand here," his father said softly. They stopped by a bulletin board, large and rectangular. Next to it was a water fountain. He saw the men with the cameras down the hallway. They were all looking away from him, toward the outside ramp and the door leading in. He turned the other way and saw a desk down at the other end. It looked empty, though there were voices off to the right, around a corner. He saw someone's hand reach for a telephone on the desk as it rang, but he only saw the arm and then his father was speaking to him.

"Be very quiet," his father said. His father's hand was on his shoulder, rubbing in a circle, gently, like a massage, but his eyes were out toward the ramp. He looked that way, too. There was a sudden flurry of activity and then

someone was coming down the ramp outside, a group of
people, and the noise level began to rise.

He saw the door open and then there was shouting and
the men with the cameras started to take pictures. There
were bright flashes. He couldn't see anyone, only a dense
mass moving slowly down the hallway toward them. His
father was gripping his shoulder, but still gently. Then he
let go, though his body was still pressed next to him. The
mass got closer and spread out, thinning; there were people
shouting, "No more! No more questions now!" and then
the group was upon them and passing. Two men walked
briskly past, looking straight ahead to the desk at the other
end of the hall. Behind them were two other men, one of
them holding the other by the arm. The other man had his
head down but he raised it slightly when he was just by
them. The man seemed to sense something. He turned and
looked and then Jack saw who it was and his mouth opened
to cry out. But then his father was pushing him back. His
father said, "Now," and then he stepped forward, deliberately and carefully, and there was something in his hand
and he held it up to the man's head and the man tried to
twist down and away but his father pulled the trigger.
There was a red flash and the man's head exploded, and
then Jack was screaming, *"Uncle Martin! Uncle Martin!"* as
the man slid to the floor and his father turned to him and
held him tight as other hands reached for them . . .

There was an insistent buzzing sound, and then the scene
receded from him and turned white. The buzz became a
ringing sound. He groaned and opened his eyes. He was in
his bed, in his undershirt and pants. It was stuffy in the
room and he felt as if the heat had been turned up. There
was sweat on the sheets where they stuck to his arms. There
was no light but the red pulse of the digital alarm clock
which threw a low crimson shadow against the telephone.

He rolled into a sitting position and pulled the ringing phone off its cradle.

His hand did not grip it well, and the phone fell, catching the edge of the bed. He fumbled it into his hand and put it to his ear.

Someone said, "Jack?"

"Yes."

"I'm sorry, I didn't think you'd be asleep."

It was her voice, Ginny's voice.

"What time is it?" he said, not looking at the digital clock.

"I thought you'd be up. It's about ten."

"I was tired." He waited for her to say something but she didn't.

"You called me," he said finally.

"Yes. I wanted to ask you something."

He waited.

Her voice was hesitant. "I'm leaving in a couple of days, and I wanted to know if I could stop by for those things I left."

Her voice went away from him. And then suddenly she was with him. He saw her there, on the bed, her hair framing her white face, her eyes unfocused, staring up at him, her mouth open, little whispers of panicky breath coming from her, her arms around him, pulling, pulling, trying, finally trying, both of them trying . . .

"Sure," he said.

"I . . . just don't think we would've worked it out."

"Impotence and frigidity aren't a very good combination . . ." He added quickly, "I'm sorry I said that. I know you tried."

"I did, Jack."

"I just thought we could have fixed it up with time, that's all."

"I know. I thought so, too. But . . ."

"Now you don't think so."

"No, I don't." Her voice was far away. He knew that later he would think about it, the tone of her voice, that it would hurt hearing it in his mind again.

He tried to lighten his voice. "Didn't meet some other goofball, did you? In a bus station or something?"

She was very silent this time. "There might be someone else."

"Might be?"

"I'm not sure, yet. Not sure if I want there to be."

"But you're going away with him to find out." The fighting tone was coming back, the dueling stance he had assumed with her so many times.

"That's not it. I'm going away to think about it. Meeting him just made me sure about you and me."

Hearing her voice like that, the fight drained out of him. "I think I know what you mean," he said.

"Do you?"

"No."

Again she was silent. Then, "Good-bye, Jack."

"Ginny?"

"Yes?"

He let the phone receiver nestle slowly into its berth. The line of electricity, the voice turned into electrons, was cut off.

"Forget it," he said.

The phone rang again almost immediately. He waited and then picked it up.

"Yes?"

"Mr. Paine?"

Not Ginny; another voice, cold, smooth and efficient.

"This is Paine."

"I'm Gloria Fulman." The name meant nothing except

something very vague, and as it came to him she added, "The former Gloria Grumbach."

"Yes, Ms. Fulman. What can I do for you?"

"I thought you'd like to speak with me."

"I'd be happy to see you tomorrow—"

"I'd like you to come to my hotel tonight."

"It's kind of late, Ms. Fulman. And I'm tired—"

"My sister is being cremated at nine o'clock tomorrow morning, and I will be leaving immediately afterward. If you'd like to speak to me it will have to be tonight."

"All right. Where are you?"

She told him, and he wrote it down.

"I'll be there in twenty minutes."

"That will be fine."

He put the phone down again, in its cradle, and stared at it before rising to his feet and pulling his shirt on.

S·I·X

The elevator rose smoothly to the fifth floor. He got off and turned left. Her suite was at the end, double-doored with a private hallway. There was a knocker on the door, and he used it. He saw the bright tiny light of the peephole darken, then the door opened.

"Come in, Mr. Paine," she said.

She was better-looking than he thought she would be. On the telephone she had sounded tall, thin and stiff, but she was short and just a little overweight, the kind of chubbiness that adds the right amount of curve to the right places. Her hair was medium short, styled high on top. She looked to be in her mid to late twenties.

She brought him into a brightly lit living room; Paine counted four other doors and an open pantry leading to a small kitchenette. She obviously liked to spend money on suites, even for one night.

"The liquor cabinet is stocked, if you'd like anything. Or I have coffee."

"Coffee would be fine."

She walked to the pantry and said something. A few moments later a young girl in a maid's uniform appeared with a tray. The service was silver; there was a platter with tea sandwiches on it.

"You don't travel light," Paine said when the maid had left.

Gloria Fulman's own coffee cup steamed untouched on the table beside her. She didn't take cream. She didn't smile.

"I have a favor to ask of you, Mr. Paine," she said.

"I'm listening."

"I want you to keep the five hundred dollars my sister gave you, plus the five hundred dollars my father gave you. I will give you five hundred dollars also. I want you to forget about the Grumbach family."

Paine said, "I can't do that. Your sister signed a contract with the agency I work for."

"I want to cancel that contract."

"Ms. Fulman," Paine said slowly, "I work for a man who won't let me do that. There are a lot of reasons. One of them is that there would be more money coming to his agency after I finished the job. Another is that he just won't let me do it."

"Would *you* do it, Mr. Paine?"

"No."

"I see."

"I don't think you do. I think you'd like to drop the whole thing because you're afraid of scandal. You'd like to shut the whole mess up now, and let it all die down, and then pick up the pieces and assemble them so that the good name of the Grumbach family goes on. And you're willing to give me a lot of money to do that. Am I right?"

"I don't know why you're so angry, Mr. Paine. So far I haven't bribed you heavily at all." He thought he detected a trace of a smile but decided that it was just a trick of the light.

"Mr. Paine, do you think my father killed himself?"

"No, I don't."

"And do you think my sister Dolores killed herself?"

"Possibly. I don't know."

"All right, Mr. Paine." He could almost see the tiny gears spinning behind her eyes. She picked up her coffee cup and sipped at it, her expression showing that it was just the right temperature for her now, that she had known all along that it would be just the right temperature at just this time.

"Is there anything I can help you with?" she said.

He took the photographs out of his pocket and gave them to her. She went through them, bunching the first three together and handing them back and then bunching the second group and handing them back.

"Do you recognize anyone in these pictures?" Paine asked her.

"I understand that money won't work, Mr. Paine," she said. "Good-bye."

Paine got up. He made a move for the door but she sat where she was, sipping at her coffee. The servant didn't appear to show him the way out.

Paine crossed the room to the door leading out of the suite. He left it open. When he reached the end of the short hallway, he turned around. Her chair was already empty. The servant girl was there, bent over, collecting the plates and cups onto the silver tray.

S·E·V·E·N

P aine got into his car and drove out of Westchester. Soon the highway lights got sparser and then
disappeared. He kept driving. He turned the
radio on and rolled the window down, and the cool night
air came into the car and washed out the stale air. He
passed a bridge but he didn't turn onto it, and soon the
glow of Westchester behind him bled down into the
horizon and was gone. He was surrounded only by darkness. Through the windshield he saw stars. He saw a bright
dot that he knew was the planet Venus. Next to it, a few
degrees away, was another, smaller dot, red, which was
Mars. *Mars comes to Venus,* he thought, *Mars fights Venus,
and then Mars goes away and everybody's dead but Venus
shines on.* War and love, the two facts of the human
condition. Never mind taxes: there was war and love, and
even after war went away love came again until Mars

reappeared. Then the whole thing started over again. He looked away from Venus and Mars.

He drove on, and soon the highway narrowed to two thin lanes and he had to watch the road all the time. There were a few other cars, lazy drivers out after rush hour, coming home from bars, going to bars. He passed one apparently very drunk driver who had been pulled crookedly onto the shoulder of the road, partially blocking the right lane, and stood outside the car arguing with a state trooper whose car flashers mixed red and white, like Mars and Venus, and who had the man leaning back against his car, his head looking up at the spinning sky. No doubt he saw something spinning not up in the sky but in the top of his head, where the alcohol had gone, where whatever it was that was meant to go away probably still lurked, waiting for a few hours of sleepy unconsciousness before creeping back up into the driver's head to torment him again. The red and white flashers disappeared around a turn in his rearview mirror.

He drove as the night got darker. There was no moon, and Mars and Venus wheeled and sank and then were gone. Over the hills and low mountains in the coming distance he saw for a moment part of the Big Dipper. In the handle of the Dipper he saw Mizar and Alcor, two close stars that circled one another. He remembered that the Big Dipper was an asterism, only part of a constellation. The constellation was called Ursa Major, but he couldn't see all of Ursa Major because most of it was hidden by the curve of the mountain. Many of the stars were faint, anyway.

He went into the mountains and then he turned off the highway. There were other roads now, often narrow, with the center line smudged out by rain and salt and winter sanding. He made a turn and there, abruptly, was a

shopping mall, with new white lines around it and lights
still on in the parking lot. There were only a few cars
parked, for night watchmen and teenagers drinking or
making out. He looked away from the lights and soon they,
too, were gone.

Another few miles and he turned onto another road and
then, immediately, he made a sharp turn onto an upsloping
gravel path. The gravel gave up, leaving hard-packed dirt,
and he found himself listening to the sound the dirt made
when the wheels rolled over it. There were trees closely
bordering the road. He kept climbing at a slow angle, but
up ahead he saw a flicker of soft light that resolved into a
square of window.

He stopped the car on a flat space, next to a small pickup.
He leaned back against the seat. He stretched, rubbing his
eyes with the flats of his palms. He looked at his watch,
holding it out toward the small square window of light in
the cottage. It was nearly two o'clock in the morning. He
got out of the car and stretched again.

He walked past the window, not looking in. There was a
narrow pathway floored with brown pine needles. He
closed his eyes for a moment because he knew he could
follow it with his eyes closed. For the first time in a very
long time, he wanted a drink so badly he would have taken
it had he had it. His hand reflexively patted the pocket of
his jacket where his flask used to be.

Eyes closed, he stood still and listened to the night:
rustles, wind sighing against trees, cold silence. He opened
his eyes and moved on. He didn't need the drink anymore,
and now the pathway opened to a field of cleared trees and
low, cropped grass with a dome in the middle of it.

He saw the glow of red light in the slit on top of the
dome, heard faint music. Someone was humming along
with the music. He looked up; the stars were achingly

beautiful, the gentle slope of the clearing making them
visible nearly down to the horizon. *Asterisms,* he thought
again. The Big Dipper was sunk low now, only its handle
visible.

He opened the corrugated metal door of the dome
gently, but it made a typical grinding noise nevertheless
and his brother turned from the eyepiece of the telescope
and looked at him. He stared through the dim red light for
a moment and then he smiled.

"Jack," he said.

"Hello, Tom." He stood by the door, feeling awkward,
then stepped in and closed it behind him. It growled again,
and then the silence of the night closed in.

"What—" his brother began, but Paine cut him off
softly.

"Just in the neighborhood, Tom."

"Sure, sit down."

There was a curved bench along the perimeter of the
dome, and Paine went to it and sat, moving a book of
charts out of the way. There was a bag of pretzels there, and
he reached in, taking one.

"Something wrong?" his brother asked.

"Just felt like coming here," he answered.

Rachmaninoff was being played on the radio, and he
flinched. The piece ended, and the announcer's muffled
voice came on. He looked up at the speakers mounted high
on the walls of the dome. Tom and he and his father had
mounted them one Saturday after picking them up on sale
at Radio Shack.

"Haven't been up here in a long time, Tom."

"I know. I almost called you a few times . . ."

"I'm sorry, Tommy."

His brother shrugged.

Paine said, "I'm just sorry it took so long."

His brother stared at an eyepiece case flipped open on the end of the bench, and Paine looked out through the slit where a line of bright and faint stars made a zigzag.

"You know . . ." Tom began.

"What?"

"I was just going to say that the place is still half yours."

"It's all yours now, Tom."

His brother shrugged. "If you ever . . ."

Paine got up. "Look, Tommy, I think maybe coming up here was a mistake."

"Bullshit."

There was anger in his brother's voice. He knew it would come and it came. Tommy glared at him, something from deep inside freeing itself to fly into his face and mouth and eyes. "That's bullshit, Jack. You came up here because you wanted to, so don't hand me any shit and run away again with your tail between your legs." He held his tongue, blood rising to his face. "There were times I hated your guts. The way you left me to deal with everything." He was unable to stop. "You acted like a fucking *baby* back then, leaving me like that. You think it was easy for me? I *know* what happened to you—but I never fucking figured out what happened to me."

Paine was on his feet. His hands were trembling. Then suddenly his arms were out, and his brother fell into them. He held his brother, and his brother held him. Something washed out of the two of them, and it was a long time before they parted.

"Jesus, Jack," his brother said.

"It's okay . . ."

"I thought all of it got buried, a long time ago, but . . ."

"I know, Tommy. You just gave me what I came here for."

There was a different kind of silence between them.

Paine sat back down on the bench, and then his eyes went to the telescope, and he said, "How's the Big Eye doing these days?"

"Had the mirror resurfaced about a year ago," his brother said. "It's as good as it ever was."

Paine got up but didn't take a step. "God, that old bastard set us up all right," he said. He was staring at one corner of the dome, looking for something on the wall that wasn't there anymore, a picture of two boys and a man, all smiling.

"Come and take a look," his brother said.

He walked to the long white tube and stood before the high end, putting his eyes to the slim tube plugging out. He covered his other eye with his hand, keeping the eye open. He saw nothing for a few seconds, and then his retina was filled with a blanket of bright pinpoints with a hard glowing core. It was like looking at a crown of perfect diamonds. It was M13, the Hercules cluster of stars, one of the most beautiful things in the sky. In a moment he was lost in it, floating into the spill of diamonds, his eyes drinking them in, his mind the mind of an eight-year-old, seeing this magnificent object for the first time.

He stood away from the telescope. "It still works."

"Why don't we close it up," Tommy said.

They capped the telescope and closed the slit. Tom gathered all the charts into a pile and turned off the red light. "I'll make coffee," he said. They closed the door of the dome, latching it with a piece of wood, and Tommy led the way back through the woods to the house. He pulled open the back door and they entered the kitchen. There was a potbellied stove in one corner, giving off faint heat. Tommy threw a couple of small logs into it. Soon its grill gave off a steady orange glow and they sat at the kitchen table while a pan of water began to boil.

"It occurs to me," Tommy said when the coffee was in their mugs, "that something must have happened to you, something else, to get you up here."

"Ginny's leaving me."

"That's news?" his brother said, and then he said, "Sorry. You mean really gone."

"Yeah."

"You want it to happen?"

"I don't know."

"Want me to tell you something, Jack?"

"Haven't you told me enough already tonight?" A trace of a smile came across Paine's face.

"I'll tell you, anyway. She was always a shit."

"I don't know about that."

His brother shrugged, and they drank their coffee. Through the windows, the night wore away, toward daybreak.

Tommy said, "She never stood by you. Not when you really needed it. She just didn't have what it takes to really stand by you."

"I don't know if I blame her for it."

His brother shrugged again.

After a while Tommy said, "I meant what I said about this place being yours when you want it. The key's in that hollowed stump we made when we were kids."

Paine nodded, looking out the window at the pink of dawn. "I've got to be leaving soon."

"Could be a good day," Tommy said quietly.

"Could be."

E·I·G·H·T

He got back down to Yonkers just before noon. His stomach was starting to grumble so he pulled off the Saw Mill Parkway, drove awhile and found a diner he knew. If he followed the road it was on, and went south, he would, after two hundred blocks, find himself in the middle of Times Square.

He ate, then drove north again and made a few turns and then he pulled up in front of Bravura Enterprises. It was a stuccoed flat-fronted building, the kind that might have been anything before it was Bravura Enterprises—a bowling alley, chemical lab, furniture outlet. The sign looked a few years old, undented metal but pigeon-spotted in places and beginning to fade.

He was surprised to find how nice the offices inside were—whoever had gutted the building had done a good job. The reception area, except for the lack of windows, might have been on the fiftieth floor of any office building on Park Avenue. The secretary also looked New York City, not the usual polyester you found in the suburbs. She had red hair that looked real. Her brass nameplate said "Mary Wagner." She smiled and told him no, he couldn't see Mr. Paterna.

Paine, returning her smile, said, "Tell Mr. Paterna that Gloria Fulman sent me."

She turned and spoke into her intercom, then swiveled back with the same liquid smile and eyes.

"He'll see you in five minutes, Mr. Paine."

After exactly five minutes he was ushered down a short, carpeted hallway into Les Paterna's office. This was nicely done also. There was some taste in evidence here, not the kind that you buy package-made from some cheesy interior decorator, but the kind that a man would execute after thinking for years and years about the way he'd really like to have things.

Paine sat down. Paterna sat down on the other side of his desk. He was a little older than his photo, early fifties. He made a steeple with his hands, a gesture which made Paine immediately dislike him.

"What can I do for you?"

Paine flipped the photo of Paterna across the desk at him, then took it back. He noticed that Paterna's nails were manicured.

"That's a picture of me," Paterna said. "It was taken about five years ago, at the Grumbach estate. So?"

Paine showed him the other two photographs. "Know these people?"

"No, I don't," Paterna said. "Is there anything specific you want to know, Mr. Paine?"

"Will you tell me how long you knew Morris Grumbach?"

"We met at a party seven or eight years ago."

"Remember whose party it was?"

"No, I don't."

"Did you work for him long?"

"*With* him, Mr. Paine. Morris and I were partners. He needed some help, and I needed some help, so we decided to make a go of it together."

"Why did you split?"

Paterna didn't blink. "We stopped needing each other."

"Was it amicable?"

"I'd have to admit that it was more my idea than Morris's. But he got over it. I'd say we were friends again by the end."

"Friends?"

Paterna smiled. "Friendly."

Paine showed him the other three photographs. For the faintest moment he thought something registered on Paterna's face.

Paterna handed the photographs back. "I don't know any of these people."

"Do you remember anything about the two younger Grumbach girls?"

Paterna drew a cigarette case out, took a short cigarette from it, didn't offer Paine one. "They were nice girls. I was over there a lot for a while. The youngest had emotional problems, but she was a nice girl." He lit the cigarette. "I was sorry to hear she killed herself."

Paine asked, "Did you call Gloria Fulman just before you let me in here?"

Paterna's eyes stared at him.

"I hope she spoke well of me," Paine said.

Paterna replied, "Is there anything else you wanted to know?"

"How's business?" Paine asked, getting up.

Paterna smiled, showing shark's teeth. "Better than yours."

Paine saw the handgun in the window of the car across the street a half second before he heard the shot. Something automatic took over his body and he dropped to the sidewalk. He heard a second shot strike overhead behind him. He crawled forward and heard another one hit the cement in front of him. A pebble of concrete flicked against his cheek.

As he reached a parked car he heard a gunned engine. He stood cautiously. The blue tail of a sedan was disappearing around a corner and then the world was quiet again.

He got into his car and drove four blocks, waited in a shopping center parking lot and then drove slowly back. He parked fifty yards from Bravura Enterprises. A half hour went by and then a blue Chrysler nosed onto the street and passed him, pulling into an empty spot a few cars ahead. There was a driver, and a man in back on the driver's side. They got out and walked up the block to the Bravura Building and went in.

The afternoon wore on. Paine turned on the car radio, low, and waited. His stomach began to growl but he ignored it. A bank of clouds came over and it looked for a time as though it would rain. The clouds broke up, letting in blue patches of sky again, and then the sky began to get dark.

At five o'clock there was a flurry of activity in front of the building. Fifteen or twenty people came out, got into various cars and drove away. Paine turned off the radio. Another ten minutes went by and then Les Paterna came out with Mary Wagner. They stopped in the doorway, and Paterna took her by the arm. He tried to kiss her but she pushed him away. Paine heard Paterna laugh, and she said something and walked away. Paterna got into the Mercedes in front of the building and drove off.

A few minutes later the two men from the blue Chrysler came out of the building. One of them got into a red Toyota, and the other walked toward the Chrysler, got in and pulled out.

Paine started his engine and followed the Chrysler, keeping well back. He got on the Saw Mill Parkway, then got onto the Taconic Parkway. He stayed on this till he got off in Croton and drove to a small house. Paine parked across the street and watched him collect his mail and go in. The mailbox said "Hartman." He saw the light go on in the front room, then saw his shadow pass by it.

It began to rain. That bank of clouds had found its way back and decided to do its business.

Paine got out of the car and went up the walk. He knocked on the door, hiding his face in his coat collar as if the rain was bothering him. The door opened.

"Mr. Hartman?" he said. "I'm here about your paperboy."

Hartman stood with his unbuttoned shirt pulled out of his pants and a beer in his hand. He had the screen door half open before he tried to pull it closed again. Paine pulled the door open and threw his weight inside, hitting Hartman in the midsection and sending him back against a stairway leading to the second floor. Hartman dropped his beer and put his hands up, but he was slow and not very good. Paine hit him once in the face and once in the stomach. He groaned and leaned back against the stairs but then he found strength and tried a weak punch at Paine's head. It missed, and Paine punched him not too hard in the groin and that was it for his resistance.

Paine pulled him by his shirt into the living room. There was only one light on; the rest of the house looked dark except for the kitchen. Paine pushed him into a square overstuffed chair and pulled up a matching chair. There was a sofa made in the same cheap square style, and a coffee table that looked like it came with the package deal. Hartman was bent over, trying to breathe.

"I didn't hit you that hard," Paine said, pushing him back up into a sitting position. Hartman looked at him as though he had hit him plenty hard.

"Where's your jacket?" Paine asked. Hartman pointed weakly to the kitchen. Paine found the jacket thrown over a straight-backed chair. He went through the pockets but found nothing. When he came back into the living room Hartman was sitting up on his own but still looked hurt.

"The other joker has the gun?" Paine asked. When Hartman said nothing Paine went over to him and balled his fist under his eyes.

"You don't tell me, I hit you in the hangers again," he said. "I used to be a cop but I'm not anymore, so I can do whatever I want to fuckheads like you and not much will happen to me."

Hartman looked surly but said, when Paine cocked his fist back playfully, "He's got the gun."

"What's his name?"

Hartman took a few breaths and then said, "Childs."

"Does he have a record?"

"Couple of years."

"What about you?"

Hartman stared at the floor. "Same."

"How long have you worked for Paterna?"

"A while."

"I don't give a shit about you," Paine said, "or about your friend, but I don't like being shot at. Not even if it's for fun. Answer the next question carefully. Do you know anything about Morris Grumbach?"

Staring at the floor, Hartman shook his head. "No."

"You never heard Les Paterna mention him?"

"I just work for Paterna. He tells me and Childs what to do. Most of the time I don't do anything. Today was the first time he ever really asked me to do something."

Paine felt like hitting him again. "Is that why you enjoyed it so much?"

Hartman was silent.

"I don't want to see your fucking face again," Paine said. "And I don't want to see your friend's face. Tell him that if I see either of you around me I'll break both your backs. You can tell Paterna that, if you want to. If you're aching to be bad boys again forget it, because you're the kind of scumbags that'll never get it right."

He went to the front hallway and looked at the spreading stain on the rug and the can lying edgewise, empty.

"Sorry about the beer," he said.

N·I·N·E

When his key was halfway in the lock he heard voices inside his apartment. He put the key all the way in and slowly turned it, then pushed the door open an inch at a time. The voices were not in the front room but somewhere in the back. Lights were on all over the place. He left the door open behind him.

He heard Ginny's voice. It went high and she was laughing. He walked into the front room and saw that the bedroom door was closed. Two coats, a man's and a woman's, were on the floor where they had missed the arm of a chair. Next to the chair was a paper bag filled with folded paper bags.

Ginny laughed, and then a man laughed. His voice was low-pitched. He laughed some more and then he said something that Paine couldn't hear. Ginny laughed again. Then there were other sounds and Ginny stopped laughing.

Paine heard her moan. The man's voice became more insistent behind the door and then Ginny was breathing loud and hard.

Paine stood frozen. He heard his own bed move, heard the creaks he heard every night when he went to sleep in it. Ginny gasped, the man grunted and then Ginny began to make little "ah" sounds in her throat. They came one after another. Paine felt numb, but despite this he began to count in his head. He counted past twenty. When he got to twenty-five Ginny's panting broke suddenly. She gave a low, strangled, painful sound in her throat. The man stopped grunting. Paine heard him say distinctly, "Are you all right?" He was still breathing heavily. Paine heard his wife begin to whimper; he could almost see her eyes now, the hunted look that was in them, seeking a way out, any way out—

The man said, "What's the matter?" and then he began to breathe rhythmically. He was trying to work against her sounds. Ginny sighed and began to make the "ah" sounds again. The "ahs" went away abruptly and then she was crying out, in short steady moans. The man breathed, "Yes yes yes."

And then the painful sound came again into his wife's throat. She said, "No!" The bed stopped moving. The man's breathing broke. He said, "What is it?" This time his voice was sharper. Ginny said, "No, no," and then Paine heard someone get up off the bed. His wife began to sob.

Paine turned and walked out of the apartment, closing and locking the door behind him.

The rain had stopped. Paine looked up through the long telescope formed by the apartment buildings around him and saw that the sky was still dark and cloudy. No Mars or Venus. But they were up there somewhere.

He left the car where it was and got on a bus. It was only nine o'clock but it was a Thursday night and the bus was almost empty. There were three girls along the back seat, in solid sweaters and new jeans and open slicker raincoats. They looked like college girls. They were laughing about something. A little later they got off. Two stops later Paine got off.

He didn't salute the night doorman because he didn't know him. He signed in and showed his ID, then took the elevator upstairs. He used his key and went in. He turned on the light in the reception area and then the hall lights, and walked down the hall to his office. He didn't open the door. The cleaning woman had left the empty refuse pail outside. He left it where it was.

He walked back up the hallway and turned on the light in Jimmy Carnaseca's office. The contraption on his desk was taller but still unrecognizable, a grid of girders that refused to take geometric shape. Paine turned off the light and walked to the end of the hallway.

He heard music. The light was off in Barker's office. Paine thought the door would be locked but it wasn't. He eased it open.

The room was empty. He saw the outline of Barker's long chair and the length of his desk. The Rachmaninoff Third Piano Concerto was still playing.

Fucking idiot, Paine thought. Barker had the tape on a loop; when the time came, a guy would come in and put another tape loop on, something like the Mozart Piano Concerto 21—classical music for people who knew nothing about it but wanted to think they did without having to listen to it.

Paine turned the light on on Barker's desk. He looked for a switch to turn the tape loop off. There wasn't one. He only found a volume dial set into the wall inside one of the bookshelves. He turned it down all the way,

which wasn't enough but at least it was low enough so
that he really couldn't tell what it was without concen-
trating. The last thing he felt like doing was concentra-
ting.

He went to Barker's couch. He bunched his jacket into a
pillow and lay down.

He pulled out the photos from his pocket and flipped
through them, one by one. Les Paterna and two other
creeps, and three pictures of barbecue folks. Who the hell
were they? He lingered on the last picture, the head-and-
shoulders shot of the man in a corporate pose. He was
smiling slightly but his eyes looked old. He looked like he
had once smiled a lot but then something had happened to
him and he had never smiled like that again. He looked
haunted.

He put the pictures back in his pocket. He got up and
turned the light on the desk off and lay down again. He
closed his eyes. As low as the Rachmaninoff was, the notes
came to him distinctly now, striking one by one on his ears.
But he was so tired it didn't matter.

Fucking idiot . . .

The world came back.

It was still dark. He held his watch up and pushed the
little button on the side that made the digital display light
up. Ten twenty-five. Now with his eyes open he saw the
blackness of night outside Barker's window. He saw a
single star. The rest were out there somewhere, fighting to
get through the buildings. The room was filled with dark
shadows. Paine yawned and then froze.

Someone was walking down the hallway tentatively. The
cleaning woman? No. Whoever it was stopped at a doorway and opened it. He heard the click of a light switch and
then another click and the close of a door. The steps
retreated.

He got up and walked to the doorway and looked out.

"Can I help you, Mrs. Meyer?"

Rebecca Meyer was out there. She still looked boyish, her hair combed to one side, a coat thrown over a tennis shirt and slacks.

She started, but quickly recovered herself. "Mr. Paine," she said. "I was looking for you." She walked down the hallway toward him. "I was told you were up here working."

"Sleeping," he said. "Who let you in?"

"The guard downstairs. He said you had signed in at nine and hadn't signed out again. I . . . thought it would be all right."

Paine went back into Barker's office and sat down on the couch. He picked his jacket up and started smoothing it out.

"What made you look for me here?"

"I called you at home. Your wife answered and said you might be here."

She knew, Paine thought. *She knew I was there.*

He snorted a laugh. "Sure."

"May I sit down?" She was standing straight in front of him.

He waved at one of Barker's interrogation chairs, but she sat next to him on the sofa.

"There was something I had to tell you," she said. She was uncomfortably close. "Mr. Paine, can I be direct with you?"

"Why not?" he answered. "Everybody else is."

"I'm attracted to you," she said, putting her hand on his arm.

"Mrs. Meyer," he said.

"My name is Rebecca."

"I don't think this is something you want to do."

He felt the heat of her hand on his arm.

"My mother taught me," she said, "never to be shy about getting what you want. It's something she taught all of us."

"So here you are," he said.

"Yes," she said. She moved her hand up his arm to the soft part of his neck and then his face. He looked into her eyes. They had the same deepness they had the first time he'd spoken to her—direct and at the same time chameleonlike—eyes he could lose himself in . . .

"What about your husband?" he said.

"Gerald is not my husband," she answered. "He used to be my husband. And your wife?"

"Over," he said.

She put her lips on his. It was as if something melted in him. Then he didn't know where he was. He became hands and eyes and mouth. His brain went away. His mouth was on her mouth and then her neck and then her throat and her breasts; his hands were helping but her clothes seemed to go away by themselves. There was nothing but the two of them. They were sitting on the couch and then they were on the floor. She was whispering to him, begging him, and he said, "I have a problem there."

Her eyes went wide and she smiled. Then the world went away again and she did something and then suddenly everything was all right.

"That's the way," she breathed. "That's it."

And then he heard only her breath.

"Why do you think your sister Gloria didn't tell me she knew Les Paterna?" he asked her. He looked at his watch; it was seven o'clock. The sun had pushed the stars out of the sky. He finished smoothing his jacket and put it on.

"Gloria was pretty chummy with Les Paterna at one time. And I was sure she'd try to hush up this thing with my father and sister."

"She already has." He told her about Hartman.

"You think Gloria told Paterna to have you shot at?"

"I'm sure she knew that if she told Paterna I was nosing around he would take care of things in his own way. She might have told him to keep a leash on it and just try to scare me."

"My sister is a bitch."

He looked at her levelly. "What do you know about Paterna?"

"I only know that he was partners with my father for a while, and that my father couldn't stand him."

"Did they ever have any obvious fights?"

"All the time. My father did most of the yelling. Paterna never stopped smiling."

"Was there blackmail involved, something like that?"

"Blackmail?"

He kept his gaze level on her. "That's what I said."

"Not that I know of."

"When you said Gloria and Paterna were chummy, did you mean they had an affair?"

"I don't think so. Paterna did some business with my sister after his break with my father. My father, of course, disapproved."

"And that mattered to your sister?"

"I already told you about Gloria."

She put her hand on his arm, but he carefully slipped his arm away. "Look," he said, "I'm sorry if it sounds like I'm grilling you, but I'd be lying if I said I thought you were telling me everything. What about the other photographs? Are you sure there's nothing else?"

"There's nothing else."

What was it about her? When he held her it was as if he'd held someone familiar and yet far away. She was like a stranger he had always known.

She stood up; just straightening her skirt she looked ready for tennis. "I should go."

"Yes."

"I'll . . . call you later."

There was awkward silence as he stared at her.

"I'll talk to you later," she said, and left.

Paine went into his own office and turned on the lights and sat down. His mind was dancing. He closed his eyes but the dancing wouldn't go away. It was like being drunk without the happy places that drunkenness would at least take you before dropping you back into the real world. He could still feel Rebecca Meyer's smooth flesh against his hands. He wanted to touch her again. But at the same time he wanted to push her away. He looked at his hands and remembered her, and then he closed his eyes and kept them closed.

At eight-thirty he dialed the phone. Someone answered and told him to wait a moment. The line cut off and music came on. *Christ, even there?* he thought. Then the music went away. There was the sound of a distant typewriter and someone said, "Bob Petty."

"Hello, Bobby," Paine said.

Petty sighed. "How have you been, Jack?"

"Not too bad. I need background on a guy named Les Paterna."

"Mind if I ask why?"

"He's a creep, but doesn't act like one. At least not anymore. I know the bastard's got a record eight blocks long."

"I'll see what I can do." Then Petty added, "Dannon's after your ass again."

"Dannon's a fuckhead."

"I saw him yesterday. He tried to get me to help reopen your case."

"And—"

"I told him to fuck himself. But I don't think that'll stop him. He wants to bring criminal charges against you."

"Jesus."

"I don't know how far he'll get. Listen, Jack . . ."

Paine waited through the silence, and finally said, "Bobby, I know what you want to ask. The answer is still, I don't know what happened. Only Dannon knows, and he says what he says."

"What's the problem with you and Dannon, Jack?"

"He was always a fuck. He never treated me like a partner. He treated me like shit. I saw him take payoffs the first day I rode with him. He never even tried to hide it from me. The last good word he said to me was, 'Want a little of this?' and when I told him no he turned to stone. He knew I wasn't bastard enough to say anything about it, but from then on he didn't trust me. I always kept an eye on my back."

"Why didn't you tell me any of this before?"

"Because then I was a fucking cop and now I'm not a cop anymore. If he tries to go civil with me I'll blow his fucking face all over the newspapers. Tell him that for me. I don't care what he thinks about me anymore, or what any other fucking cop thinks about me, including you, Bobby, if you want to know."

"All right, Jack, take it easy. I just thought you should know."

"I appreciate it, Bob." He took a long breath. "I do."

"You've still got a few buddies over here."

"Name another one."

"I'll get back to you about this Paterna creep," Petty said, and hung up.

There came a knock at the door. Paine looked up to see Jimmy Carnaseca standing there.

"Morning, Jack," he said.

Paine held up a tired hand in greeting.

"You look like shit," Carnaseca said. "What you need is sex."

Paine stared at him.

"Don't you want to know how I've been, Jack?"

"How've you been, Jimmy?"

"Just fine. Listen," he said, fiddling with the strap of his camera bag, "you really should try one of these hubby-cheater things. You never can tell what's going to happen."

"What happened, Jimmy?"

Carnaseca winked and walked past him. "Never mind. You really *do* look like shit." He laughed and went down the hall.

T·E·N

The lights were still on in his apartment. He opened the door loudly, letting it swing back against the doorstop with a bang, then closed it and went in. The bags were gone from the side of the chair. There was only one coat there now. He heard movement in the bedroom.

She was leaving the room as he walked in.

"Oh!" she said. "I thought I heard someone at the door." She smiled uneasily. "How are you?"

She was wearing a denim skirt and a turtleneck top that showed the outline of her small waist and breasts.

He shrugged. "And you?"

"I'm okay. I hope you don't mind me taking those things . . ."

"Good a time as any. Should I leave?"

"No, of course not. I'm . . . almost finished."

"That's good."

"Why don't you . . . make some coffee or something? I'd like some."

"All right."

He went into the kitchen. He heard her hurrying through the bedroom. When he came out with two mugs and set them on the coffee table, she had four bags filled with clothes and a couple of garment bags laid neatly across the arm of the chair with her coat.

"You'll need help," he said.

"I've—" she began again. "Someone is coming up to help me."

He gave her the coffee and sat. She perched on the thin arm of the chair with the garment bags on it. She didn't look at him. He found himself thinking again about her moving under him, trying, her eyes going from moist to rock-hard, the fright in the corners filling them up—

"I don't know what I'm supposed to say," she said.

"Neither do I."

"Jack . . ." she said, trying to make herself sound reasonable, "I really don't know if this is a good way to end things."

"It's as good a way as any."

"Do you have to be cryptic? You always sound so cynical about everything."

He said nothing.

"Jack," she said, "I guess what I'm trying to say is that I wish it had worked out. I think I'll always wish that."

"Always?"

"Yes."

"As long as it was both our faults, I guess that's okay."

Something changed in her face. He knew he had chipped away a piece of her.

"Ginny," he said, "I'll always feel that you thought, deep down inside, that almost everything was my fault."

"Yes, that's true."

"Can you tell me why?"

"Because you didn't have to do the things you did. You could have been better than what you are."

"I don't understand, Ginny."

Her face began to change. The self-consciousness was gone; it was as if she had realized that this was the last time she would be able to say these things.

"Goddammit," she said. "What do you think it was like living with you? I never knew what the hell you were going to do. Every time I talked to you I didn't know which Jack I was going to get—the happy one, the one in a black mood, the wiseass one or . . ."

She bit her lip.

"Or what?"

"The one with the gun to his head! Don't you think I knew about the box of shells in the kitchen cabinet? Goddammit, Jack!" She began to cry.

She stood up and gathered her things. She threw her coat over her arm, scooping the bags of clothes into her two hands. "I've got to go."

"Can't I help you?"

"I'll . . . meet him downstairs. I've got to go."

She opened the door and walked out.

He rose and put his hand on the door. He stood with it open, listening for the elevator, and then it came. The elevator doors kissed shut and he heard it go down.

Behind him, the telephone rang.

"Jack?" Bob Petty's voice said.

"Yeah."

"Are you okay? You sound strange."

"I'm all right. You have something on Paterna?"

"Sort of. Paterna is dead."

A slight chill rose up Paine's back as Petty went on.

"He hung himself in his bedroom. His girlfriend found him about three this morning. She says they had a fight and she sent him home alone last night."

"Was there a suicide note?"

"No. That's one of the reasons we're holding the girlfriend. But there's something else funny. I started poking around and hit a brick wall on this guy. There wasn't any Les Paterna seven years ago."

"He was a wash job?"

"New name, new face. Probably a federal witness."

"Thanks, Bobby."

"No problem. You sure you're okay?"

"Yeah."

"Want to shoot some pool tonight?"

"I'm all right, Bobby."

"Remember what I said about Dannon."

"I will. Thanks."

He hung up.

E·L·E·V·E·N

He was in the second bad place.

Again, it was more a feeling that it would get bad because it didn't start that way. He was with Tom, and they were in the woods. For the first time in a long time it was like it had been. He was home. He had his uniform on. Tom had a beard and long hair. The air in the woods smelled good, and it was getting late in the day. He always liked this time. He had his coat off and if it had been just a little warmer he would have taken his shirt off, too. He had an axe in his hands. He swung it in long high arcs and it felt good coming down on the wood. The wood made a good clean sound when it split.

"Been a long time since I did this," he said.

"Bet they had you doing plenty of other shit in the Army," Tom said.

"Like peeling potatoes? Not much."

Tom fiddled with the radio resting on a tree stump. He

glided through channels until he found a station playing loud rock and roll.

"What the hell band is that?" Jack asked, indicating the music that was on.

"Crosby, Stills, Nash and Young."

"Didn't they used to be in different bands?"

"Now they're playing together. Like it?"

Jack nodded. "I haven't heard much of anything the last six months."

Tom put the chain saw he was oiling down. "You think you'll end up over there?"

"They say it'll be over by next summer."

"If Nixon wins in the fall. I know they're holding up those peace talks till after the election."

"I don't think about it anymore. The news is we won't end up in Nam even if it doesn't end. They're pulling so many guys out now they wouldn't have anybody for us to relieve. I'll probably end up at Fort Bragg. Maybe in Germany." He looked at the head of the axe, then put it down on the tree stump next to the radio. "You want to hear some real news? I've got a girlfriend."

Tom grinned. "You're kidding."

"I'm serious."

"You must be. You never told me about any of the others."

"This one is for real."

"How long have you known her?"

"I met her three weeks ago."

"Three weeks! Christ, you hardly know her."

"I've got a good feeling about her, Tommy. We've talked about getting married."

"Jesus!"

"Her name is Ginny. I'll bring her around." Jack picked up the axe and swung it into the wood.

They piled the cut logs and covered the pile with a tarp. Then Tom pointed to the sky. "Better get going before it gets dark. I'm tired, anyway."

"Give me one minute," Jack said, sitting on a stump. "I wanted to ask you about Dad."

"What's to say?"

"He looked like shit when I saw him yesterday down at the house. Doesn't he do anything?"

Tom made himself busy packing the chain saw and its gas. "No."

"Does he give you any trouble?"

"He sits and watches TV, or stares at the walls."

"What the hell did they do to him in that place?"

His brother looked at him with annoyance. "Haven't you ever thought about it? What do you think they did to him? They kept him in there. All his problems are in his own head. That's what the trouble is." He turned back to the chain saw, snapped it into its case.

"I think about him all the time," Jack said.

"He talks about you. You're all he talks about."

"What does he say?"

"What do you fucking *think* he says? He talks about what happened to you. He talks about what he did."

"Isn't there any way to make him forget?"

"How? He shot his own fucking brother in the head— and he thinks you hate him for it. How are you going to make him forget that? Did *you* forget it?"

They walked back to the house. They stacked some wood against the wall and went in.

The phone rang, and Jack picked it up.

"Jack," his father said. It was a stranger's voice. It was as if pain itself was talking, using the old man's voice.

"Dad, what is it?"

"I'm going," his father said.

"Da—"

"Mizar and Alcor, Mizar and Alcor in the handle of the Big Dipper. Two stars, Jack. Brother and brother."

"Dad, what the hell's wrong?"

"Forgive me, Jack. Love your own brother. Oh, Jesus—"

There was a sound over the phone that was louder than anything he had ever heard. His mind went on fire. For a moment he thought the phone had exploded in his hand. Then he knew what the sound was—he had heard it in the Army. He had heard it that day in the police station, when his father had raised his hand—

He screamed "No!" into the phone, and then he kept on screaming.

"Oh, Jesus."

He sat up on the couch. He had sweated right through his shirt and jacket. There was a dull ache behind his eyes; it was as if the projector was still on and the pictures he had seen were still there after the lights had gone up. His palms were wet.

He rose and went to the window. It was still midday. There was some sun but mostly there was just gray where he looked down toward the street. Gray sunlight.

He wished he had Rebecca Meyer with him. But the thought turned sour in him immediately. He was glad she wasn't with him.

Gray sun. The day would go on and then the world would darken to gray night. Tomorrow the sun would come up and the world would be gray again.

He went to the kitchen and filled a glass with water. It went down his throat like bile, sticking to the roof of his mouth instead of washing down the bile that was already there. He nearly threw the glass but instead placed it very gently on the counter. He walked to the bedroom.

The closet was still open. He saw that there was a dress that Ginny had left. It was white and black, white with large black dots on it. He didn't recognize it. He could not remember ever seeing her in it. Had he ever really looked at her in anything? He couldn't remember. There was that one sweater, the one a little like the one that girl on the bus was wearing, a shade of rose that was neither red nor pink. It was the first time he had looked at Ginny's breasts. The sweater wasn't tight but still it showed her breasts off through the wool. That was the second time he had seen her. What had she worn the first time? He didn't know.

He turned from the closet and sat on the bed for a moment, his hands heavy on his knees. Then he moved one hand to the small table beside the bed. There was a long drawer, and he slid it open, pulling it all the way out until the weight of what was in it started to push the drawer down and threatened to pull it out of the table.

There was only one thing in the drawer. He took the gun out and let it sit in his hand. It had the weight of a dead bird. It was cold and blue, the blue of metal. He closed his eyes and it still felt like a bird in his hand.

He remembered a time when he was drunk, before he had given up drinking. He had been at it all night, had started after getting off duty. This night it had done nothing but sharpen what was in his head. He had taken in so much Scotch that it meant nothing to his body. The one part of his mind that he wanted the liquor to kill had become sharp and bright as lightning. Bobby Petty had driven him home and then left. He knew that Petty hadn't been drunk because Petty never got drunk, and because he had started to get on him for drinking so much.

After Petty left, he sat at the kitchen table, waiting for the lightning in his head to go away. It stayed bright. He sat there for a long time. Then he looked down and his gun was in his hand. There were bullets scattered over the kitchen table. He had taken the bullets out of the gun, but there was still one in it.

It was then that he closed the cylinder and spun it, and put the gun to his temple. He felt nothing. Suddenly the lightning in his head flashed out and all he could feel was his finger on the trigger of the gun. No other part of him was alive. He felt the pressure on his finger, nothing else. His finger was alive, filled with electricity; the rest of him was dead storm. He felt the pressure against the finger grow. The finger was living for him, a lightning bolt, doing everything for him. No other part of him had to think, or eat, or breathe.

Then something (his finger?) made him look up. Ginny was standing in the doorway to the kitchen in her bathrobe. Her eyes were not wide because he had caught her at the exact moment when her eyes first made contact with him. None of the things that should be were in her eyes, the disbelief, the screams, the pleading for him to stop. Nothing was there but her first pure reaction, which was—*get it over with.* There was relief in her eyes in that unadulterated, frozen moment—relief that it would happen now and not some other night, or day, not while he was on duty or in a bar or by himself in a hotel room with a razor in front of a fogged mirror, with only silver and white the colors of the world, the white and silver of the bathroom and the white of his undershirt and underwear, staring at his own face while the silver razor did the job, and she would have to go somewhere to look at his body with all that blood on it. They wouldn't clean the blood off, and his undershirt would be caked with it, and his face would have the lusterless pallor of a stranger. *Let it happen now,* her eyes said. *Get it over with.*

In that moment he knew he didn't love her, if ever he

had. There was no possibility of loving her because she did not love him.

Then suddenly his finger gave up its life to him. The storm ended. He felt everything again.

She walked to him and put her hand on the gun and pressed it to the kitchen table. She held it against the Formica. "I'll get you a cup of coffee," she said.

She made coffee, and he drank some, and while she was putting the cups in the sink he opened the cylinder of the .38 and saw the single bullet stare up at him from the chamber that would have fired.

He sat on the bed in the gray afternoon and looked at the gun in his hand now. There was no more alcohol and no more Ginny. But the same numbness was there that was always there, without the alcohol or with it. It had never gone away. That was what had put the gun in his hand, not the beer or scotch, or the fact that his wife didn't love him, or that his father had killed himself. There was still the fact that it was his own choice. When his finger was doing the job that night, the finger was him. His mind could produce all the metaphors it wanted, confuse them, change them around, but it would still be him. He knew that. But it made no difference because the numbness was still there.

He felt the weight of the gun in his hand. He slipped his fingers around the butt in a smooth motion and put his finger onto the trigger, feeling where it should go. Then he put the barrel to his temple and pulled the trigger.

"Bang," he said.

The gun said *click*.

He took the barrel away from his head and turned the gun over and put it slowly back into the drawer, more carefully than he had handled the water glass in the kitchen, and he closed the drawer, and then he changed his shirt and jacket and went out into the gray world of sun.

T·W·E·L·V·E

In the gray jail cell, Mary Wagner looked shorter than she had standing with Les Paterna outside Bravura Enterprises. That was because Les Paterna had probably been shorter than he had looked behind his desk. Another businessman with deceptive interior decorating.

He would have to ask Barker if there was a listing in the Yellow Pages for magic furniture that turned creeps into big shots.

"How did you get in?" Mary Wagner asked him. She had been crying. Her mascara was smeared all around her eyes, giving them a haunted look. Up close, her hair coloring was apparent, the soft red locks giving way to mousy brown at the roots. Altogether, she didn't look as New York professional as he had thought. Trick lighting, no doubt.

"I told them I was your lawyer. The guard barely looked at me. He was arguing with his wife on the phone."

She looked at him and didn't even pretend to smile.

"Do you have a lawyer?" he asked her.

"I've got one," she said. "He's the Bravura Enterprises lawyer, Henry Kopiak." She was making nervous motions with the fingers of her right hand; the nicotine-stained place between her middle and forefinger was empty and she was obviously not used to that.

"Sorry, I don't have a cigarette," he said.

Abruptly, she began to cry.

"I had a fight with him," she sobbed, the way people do when they wish they had done one little thing differently which would have saved them from a big hole they had fallen into. "That was all. He was a pain in the ass sometimes, and last night he just got on my nerves. He picked me up at nine, we had a couple of drinks, then we went back to my apartment. He started to bother me, so I kicked him out." She wiped her hand across one eye, showing Paine the technique she had used to smear her mascara.

"Did you call him later?"

She gave him a look as if he really was a lawyer.

Paine waited.

"Yes," she said.

"What time?"

She hesitated. "I'm pretty sure it was around one-thirty."

"Pretty sure?"

"I kicked him out around midnight. I gave him time to get home, and a little more time to steam. I called him because I didn't want him mad at me."

"Because he was your boss?"

She looked at him, and a sob came.

"Do you think he killed himself?" Paine asked.

Again she smeared her mascara. "Oh, God, I don't

know. I don't think so. He never talked that way. But I didn't know him all that well. He didn't tell me everything . . ."

"Did he tell you anything about the Grumbachs?"

"Only the business things. He never talked about much of anything."

"Did he ever talk about what he did before Bravura Enterprises?"

"He used to talk about it sometimes. But I got the impression he didn't like to. Like it was something to forget."

Paine took the two envelopes of photos from his pocket. He took the photographs out and handed them to her. She stopped at one of the three Dolores Grumbach had left for him, of a thin-faced man in his mid-forties with receding hair and long sideburns.

"That's Lucas Druckman; Les used to talk about him."

"Did you ever meet him?"

"No. Les kept a picture of him. He showed it to me once, after he'd had a few drinks. He told me that if I ever saw Lucas Druckman I should run the other way. He thought it was funny. He said it a couple of times."

"He thought it was funny?"

"He thought it was hilarious. He'd had a lot to drink . . ." She looked as though sobs were on the way again.

"Where did he have this picture?"

"He took it out of his desk." She moved her hand in front of her, remembering. "It was under the hanging files in the file drawer. I remember him pushing a bunch of them back to get at it. It was in a brown folder."

"Was there anything else in the folder?"

"I remember seeing some papers, maybe another picture."

Paine took the photos back from her and showed her the ones from the other envelope. They drew a blank. He took the photos back and then he called out through the cell bars, waiting for the jailer with the nagging wife to let him out.

"I don't think you have anything to worry about," he said to Mary Wagner. "If this lawyer Kopiak is any good, you'll be out in an hour. If he isn't any good, you'll be out in two hours."

A little light rose in her eyes; that was all she wanted to hear. Already she was beginning to realize how messy she looked; and Paine knew that after he left she would straighten her face and comb her hair. Pretty soon she'd be back out in the big bad world, and it would be time to be hired by some other middle-aged bozo who wanted a secretary who wouldn't mind looking up at him with round brown eyes, and show just enough leg to promise that leg led to thigh. And if her hair wasn't really red but mouse-brown, so what, it looked just fine in night light and that's all she needed. By the time the jailor arrived she was almost smiling.

Paine ate at the diner on Broadway and 250th Street, then he had more coffee and read the paper and waited for it to get very dark. When it got very dark he paid his check and left.

He parked three blocks from Bravura Enterprises and scouted carefully for the blue Chrysler or red Toyota. Neither was there. The door to the building was locked but it was an easy lock.

Once inside, he went past Mary Wagner's desk and down the hall to Paterna's office. He closed the door behind him. The blinds were already drawn so he turned on the desk light.

The file drawer in the desk had a lock on it, but that broke with only a penknife. Paterna's furniture wasn't so magical after all. Paine pushed back the blue hanging file folders and saw nothing. He rammed the folders back farther, and there, pushed to the back edge of the file, was a brown folder.

As he slid it forward and pulled it out, it slipped from his fingers and fell onto the rug, flipping open to show an empty interior.

"Shit," Paine said.

He picked the folder up and slid his fingernail along the edges. There was no split where something had been hidden. He tore the folder down the middle, telling himself that doing so was not frustration but a final check for a hiding place.

The folder turned into a ripped folder.

Paine threw the pieces into the trash can next to the desk. He started to push the file drawer closed, then stopped. He pushed the hanging folders back again, straining his fingers to the back of the drawer, sliding them from side to side. At first there was just smooth cool metal. Then his fingers found a slip of paper and he pulled it out.

One side was empty; on the other was scrawled the name Izzy, the number 33,000 and a Los Angeles phone number.

Paine put the slip of paper in his pocket and left the office. He turned out the light behind him.

T·H·I·R·T·E·E·N

Outside Paine's door someone moved in the shadows. He turned, ready, but it was Rebecca Meyer.

"You didn't answer your phone," she said.

"I wasn't home," Paine said. He opened the door for her and she went in. As she passed, something stirred in him, deep down. It was something primal, animal, but it wasn't only sexual. It both frightened and elated him.

She took off her coat. Her hair was more feminine today, brushed back from a center part. She looked older. She was wearing makeup. Her tennis togs were gone, replaced by slacks and a loose cotton blouse that didn't hide the fact that she was not wearing a bra. Paine thought of Ginny, the sweater she had worn, the one that had shown off her breasts.

He decided he had a thing about breasts.

"Do you have anything to drink?" she asked, sitting in one of the armchairs that had held Ginny's bags the day before.

"Ginger ale," he said, turning to get her one from the kitchen before she could say that's not what she meant.

When he turned from the refrigerator with the can, she was standing in front of him. She moved closer. Her face was flushed, through her makeup, as if she had played hard tennis and enjoyed it. Her eyes were filled with intelligence that had been sublimated by something more basic, a human drive that was the basis of life itself.

She took the can from him and he didn't see where she put it.

He didn't need her help this time. There was no laughter between them, no wordplay; there was something frighteningly elemental and unavoidable that removed them from the realm of human debate and made them part of nature. For the first time since he was a young boy and had lain out on the grass under the clouds, imagining himself one with those clouds, moving east with them through the thin pure blue air out to sea, he forgot who he was. He was not Jack Paine but a process, a force like the clouds or wind. There was no thought or time attached to what he was—he was outside thought or time. He was both bathed in release and horribly frightened.

Sometime during the night, it ended, and he became Jack Paine again.

She lay on the bed, and he lay next to her, and there were two of them again instead of one.

Paine stared at the ceiling. "How long did you wait for me outside the door?"

She shrugged, distracted. The flush had receded from her

face. She turned gently away from him on the bed, slipping one hand under her head and staring at the window, away from him. For a moment he thought she had fallen asleep.

"I don't know if I'm in love with you or not," she said.

If she had said it a different way, Paine might have laughed. But the way she spoke, as if her mind was as unsure as her body had been sure, made him say instead, "Does it matter?"

She shrugged, or maybe it was a shudder.

"I never loved Gerald," she said.

"That's easy to believe."

"I don't know if I've ever really loved anybody, except maybe Dolores." She spoke almost to herself.

Paine let her have silence.

"When we were little girls, Dolores and I played together when she wasn't reading. We had a cat then, and we dressed him up like he was a baby. Dolores was the father and I was the mother. I had to cook on a toy wooden stove I'd gotten one Christmas. I always had to make turkey, because that was Dolores's favorite meal. We always had it on Thanksgiving and then on Christmas, and Dolores said if we had it all the time then it would always be Christmas. I had a toy ironing board, and a little toy iron from F.A.O. Schwarz that really plugged into the wall and got a little warm on the bottom. I had to iron clothes for the cat, and I had to clean and make dinner. My mother never did those things because we had servants for all that, but in our game that was the way we did it.

"As the father, Dolores would come home from her job, and I would lay out the turkey dinner on our play table, with a real little red checkered tablecloth on it, and with plastic vegetables and even plastic cranberry sauce. Dolores would get my father's *Times* from the morning and read it at the table. She even had one of my father's old pipes, and she pretended to smoke it after the meal was finished. We always had chocolate cake for dessert, because Dolores liked it. She had chocolate cake every birthday, with chocolate icing. I fought with her sometimes, because I wanted to be the father and try the pipe and read the paper, but she never let me."

She turned her head on the pillow and lay staring at the ceiling, her face suffused with what looked like dreams. Paine watched the track of a single tear ride the corner of her eye down into the trimmed, unbrushed wave of her hair.

"I think she got it all from books," Rebecca said, and then she was quiet for a time before she rolled to Paine like a weeping child.

He held her, felt his hands around her and wanted to take whatever was gnawing through her and tear it out and kill it and then take the ripped pieces of her and fit them back together again. He had never felt like this before.

"I think I'm in love with you," he said.

"Don't say that," she sobbed gently, and he continued to hold her.

At the end of the night, he awoke and looked at her. Sleep, or what they had done, or his words, perhaps, or her words, had loosened the spring that had been wound so tight within her, and had left her limp and free to dream. Her head lay on the side of the pillow, her mouth slightly open. The hollows around her closed eyes, the dark circles of makeup, made her look as if her eyes would be larger than they were. He studied the curve of her nose, the artistic sculpture of her cheek leading to the firmer flesh of her chin and down into the valley of her throat. He thought about how few times in a man's life he was able to study a woman without her knowledge or consent, as merely a work of art.

He watched the coming light through the window play across the landscape of her face, until some relay switched within her and she stirred. She opened her eyes at him, still in her dream or just coming through its portal back into life, and for the tiniest of moments he felt on the verge of revelation. It was like the time Ginny had come into the room as he cocked the gun to his head, the frozen second of time that had forever colored her for him and opened her secret heart to him. It was like that, only it was different, and for the briefest measure of time he was on the edge of knowing what made him feel the way he did about her, and then it was lost to him. It was in his consciousness and then it was gone before he could grasp and know it.

Then her eyes really saw him, and without moving her head she smiled, and then she stretched beneath the covers.

"What time is it?" she asked.

"About seven."

Keeping her smile, she reached her hand to lay it on his arm. "I have to be at the house at nine. Lawyer business."

He brought his own arm out of her light grip. "Did your father ever mention anyone named Lucas Druckman?"

"No."

He reached over to the floor and picked up his jacket, taking the slip of paper he'd found in Paterna's office and handing it to her. "Did he ever mention someone named Izzy?"

She shook her head.

"Did your father have any business in California?"

"Nothing that I know of."

Paine reached back into the jacket pocket and retrieved the photo of the older couple with the horse. "Those are eucalyptus trees," he said, pointing to the stand of California conifers bordering the pasture in the photo. "And the phone number on that slip of paper is a Los Angeles number." He took out the picture of the head shot in sideburns. "And that's Lucas Druckman."

She looked at him. "I don't understand."

"All this has something to do with California. Does your sister Gloria have any dealings on the West Coast?"

"I don't think so. Her husband might. He's a budding politician, you know." She gave a slight smile. "He wants to be President."

Again she lay her hand on his arm, squeezing it. "If I want to see you again, do I wait outside your door?"

Paine laughed. "If you want. If you can't find me, there's a fellow named Bob Petty who might know where I am." He gave her Petty's number.

"I've got to go," she whispered.

She slipped silently out of bed and went to the bathroom. When she came out, she was dressed.

He lay in bed, looking at her. The angle of morning sun made a partial shadow of her face.

"How did your mother die?" he asked quietly.

Her face went deeper into shadow. "The death certificate my father bought said cardiac arrest. But she took an overdose of sleeping pills. She killed herself."

The shadow receded; a cloud outside the window moved away from the sun. Occluded light leapt back into her face.

"I have to go," she said.

F·O·U·R·T·E·E·N

M argie said, "Henry Kopiak is in your office."
"Shit," said Paine.
On his way down the hall, Jimmy
Carnaseca called to him from his office, and Paine went in.

"How you doing, Jack?" Jimmy smiled. He had the box
of little wooden girders out, and he was fitting one of them
precisely into the growing structure on his desk.

"Any guesses?" Jimmy asked. "You should be able to
figure it out by now."

There was an Italian architect who designed things like
this, all angles. It looked a little like a temple Paine had
seen once in *National Geographic.* It looked a little like a lot
of things.

"It's an office building," Paine said.

"Not even close," Jimmy answered, grinning. He fit
another tiny girder into its slot. "You know, Jack," he said,
"you still look like shit. Worse, even."

"Thanks."

"I still say you should do like me. What you need is more sex."

"Don't you ever work, Jimmy?"

"All night, Jack." He laughed, picking another tiny bit of wood from its box, examining it carefully, applying a dab of glue to it before wedging it between two struts.

Paine reached out to turn the model's box over and look at the picture, but Jimmy clamped his hand down.

"No fair, Jack," he said.

When Paine walked into his office, Kopiak was standing with his hands behind his back, looking out the window. He had opened the blinds, but had done it without soiling his fingers with the dust.

Kopiak's briefcase stood upright next to the visitor's chair, and his raincoat was hung neatly on the hook on the back of the door.

"What can I do for you, Mr. Kopiak?" Paine asked.

Kopiak turned and frowned, then nodded. His face was smooth and full, the kind that would turn jowly without exercise. His hair was stylishly long and gray. His clothes weren't cheap but he looked like a suburban lawyer. He looked like the kind of man who didn't like dust, but didn't mind disturbing things.

"You're certainly the Jack Paine that Mary Wagner described to me," Kopiak said. "At least you're who you say you are." A grim smile flirted with his face but lost out to the frown. He left the window and sat in the visitor's chair, and Paine sat behind his desk. Kopiak didn't reach for his briefcase immediately, which to Paine was a good sign.

"I don't approve of your impersonating me, Mr. Paine," Kopiak said. The frown deepened to borderline scowl.

"I was just doing my job, Mr. Kopiak."

"There are other ways you could have gone about it."

"Would *you* have let me in there to see her?"

"No, I wouldn't have."

"I hope you see my point, Mr. Kopiak."

"I wonder if your employer, Mr. Barker, would see it that way."

Paine shrugged.

"You could have hurt Ms. Wagner's case by prompting her to reveal information she had withheld from the police."

"Aren't lawyers supposed to keep people from incriminating themselves?"

"That's not the point, Mr. Paine."

"Did you get her out of jail?"

"Certainly I did—"

"Why don't you tell me why you came here then, Mr. Kopiak? If you wanted to slap me on the wrist about practicing law without a sheepskin, you would have called me on the phone or had me arrested. Why didn't you have me arrested?"

Kopiak glared at him.

Paine said, "You don't like me, do you, Kopiak? I certainly don't like you."

Kopiak took a deep breath and shook his head. He pulled his briefcase onto his lap and snapped it open. It was neat and tidy and he lifted a slim envelope out of a trimmed leather pocket and handed it over to Paine.

There was no writing on the envelope; it was uncreased and flat. The flap was tucked in and Paine pulled it open and lifted a blue rectangular check out.

"The check is endorsed to you, personally, for five thousand dollars, Mr. Paine. Mr. Barker needn't know about it. If you would prefer, we can go through the agency. It makes no difference to me."

"What do you want for all this money, Mr. Kopiak?"

"I want the material from the folder Mary Wagner mentioned to you, the one that was in Les Paterna's desk. I found the torn pieces of the folder in Paterna's wastebasket, which means that you were there and found it empty. Someone was obviously there before you. I'd like you to find that material and return it to me."

"Would you like to tell me what's in it?"

"No, I would not."

Paine slipped the check back into the envelope and tucked in the flap. The envelope was creased now, and he liked that. "You take this out to Margie Miles at the front desk, and she'll help you fill out one of our standard contracts. She'll also help you sign over the check to the Barker Agency. If you want to do that, I'll be glad to look for your material."

Kopiak produced a business card from another leather pocket in his briefcase and handed it to Paine. "If you find anything, call me." He snapped his briefcase shut and got up. He walked to the door and took his raincoat off the hook and draped it over his arm.

"Good-bye, Mr. Paine," he said, and left without looking back.

Paine pulled the phone in front of him on his bare desk, pulled out the slip of paper that said "Izzy" on it and dialed the California telephone number.

It rang for a long time. Then someone picked up the receiver and a woman's drowsy voice said, "What?" When Paine asked for Izzy she told him to wait. There was a long wait. Paine heard argument in the background. The phone sounded like it was picked up and then put down again. Finally, a man's voice said into it tentatively, "Hello?"

"Izzy?" Paine asked.

"Who's this?"

"I'm calling for Lucas Druckman."

There was a tiny intake of breath, and for a moment Paine thought he had hung up. Then the voice said slowly, as if it wanted to remember everything about his answer, "Who is this?"

"A friend of Lucas Druckman."

There was more argument between the two voices on the other end of the phone, then the voice came back. "Druckman had no friends."

Paine looked at the number on the slip of paper, 33,000, and repeated it into the phone.

There was a new intake of breath, a big one. The voice said, "Who gave you that figure?"

Paine played the fear in the voice. "Druckman gave it to me."

"When?"

"Recently."

"Bullshit."

"Why is that bullshit?"

Paine heard the female in the background yelling at Izzy to hang up. He kept telling her to shut up. "I'll take care of it!" he shouted, and she answered, "Shit you will." It sounded like an exchange they had often.

Izzy's voice came back to Paine.

"Who are you?"

"A friend—"

"I'll tell you," Izzy interrupted. His words trembled with suppressed fear. "I don't know who gave you that figure, or what you did to get it, but that was between Druckman and me."

Paine heard the female yell something loud and Izzy's voice shouted back at her and the phone went dead.

Paine called the number back and let it ring for five minutes. Nobody answered. He pictured the two of them, Izzy a short punk with a spreading bald head, the woman a frowzy blonde in her fifties with thick legs, the two of them packing suitcases, Izzy stopping every minute or so to say to her maybe it was just a joke, maybe it didn't mean anything, and the frowzy blonde yelling at him to remember what happened to what's-his-name, what happened when he didn't pay and thought he could get away with it, why didn't you pay Druckman, why didn't you do this and that, and then Izzy continuing to pack, the woman throwing things into suitcases now, imagining the knock at the door, imagining herself dead, a stupid old bleached blonde hooked up with an asshole named Izzy, her whole life reeling across the back of her eyes as she jammed black negligees into a suitcase and, down at the bottom, hidden, Dr. Scholl's footpads for her aching feet and a girdle she wore when they went out, which was almost never, anyway, but if Izzy knew she wore a girdle and Dr. Scholl's footpads he might dump her, even though he was an asshole, what would she do then, and Izzy pausing again, saying, "Maybe—"

Paine dialed Bob Petty. Someone told him that Petty wasn't there. He was about to hang up when Petty got on the phone.

"Glad you called, Jack."

He sounded tired and mad.

"Something wrong, Bobby?"

"Some asshole over here decided I shouldn't talk with you. I can handle it. Dannon's been on my case, just like I told you."

"You're the only guy I'd back off for, Bobby. Just ask."

He could almost hear Petty's back stiffen. "Fuck you," he

said. Then he added, "Hold on, Jack, let me take the call in an empty office."

Paine heard emptiness, then Bobby came back on. He sounded like he was in another country; the usual background of typewriters and voices was gone.

Petty said, "Dannon's bringing the whole thing out again." Petty emphasized the word "whole."

"I told you I'd chuck it," Paine said.

"And I said fuck you. It's just that it was hard enough on Terry the first time around. She still thinks all the grief I got after backing you caused the miscarriage. And now to drag it all into the open again—"

"She's pregnant?" Paine interrupted. He knew there were only a few things that would get Petty to go on like this.

"Yeah," Bob answered. He laughed gruffly. "You know she always wanted three."

She would have had them hung between the words.

It would do no good to give in to Dannon. If he tried to do that, Bobby would scream and kick his butt until they both called Dannon and told him to fuck himself. Petty was marine stock, and Irish, and nothing could get him to change his mind. If he thought Paine was giving up on something because of him, it would be worse for everybody —for Paine, for Terry, for Bobby himself. He could almost hear Petty berating himself for letting any emotion show.

"Why did you call, Jack?"

"There's another creep, named Lucas Druckman. A loan shark, probably. He's from California, might be here now."

"I have a friend named Ray at LAPD." There was silence, then Bobby said gingerly, "You know, if Dannon gets his way, it's going to open all the holes up for you again."

"I know that."

"All of them, Jack."

"Yeah."

"What I mean is . . ."

"Will I fall apart? Try to kill myself?"

"Well . . ." Two beats of silence. "Don't forget I'm here for you, if you need me."

"Don't worry about me, Bobby."

Another beat of silence. "Let me go punch out that bastard who said I wasn't here."

"Do that, Bobby."

Paine sat staring at the phone. There was a noise at the door and he looked up to see Margie. She wore her typical pained expression.

"He wants you," she said.

"My body or mind?"

Margie smiled grimly and turned back to the reception area.

The music in Barker's office was still Rachmaninoff, but the tape loop had been changed. Now it was Variations on a Theme by Paganini. A big showstopper in pop classical concerts. It was another piece that Paine liked, and now, he knew, would come to hate.

Fucking idiot.

As he sank into the chair opposite Barker the tape ended. Then, seconds later, it started again.

"You're going to Boston," Barker said, staring out the window at a place above Paine's head. "Gloria Fulman wants to talk to you."

"Why can't she talk to me on the phone?"

Barker affected disinterest. "Because that's what she wants. She's paying for it."

"She's not a client."

"She is now."

"Did she sign a contract, or just buy you?"

Now Barker looked at him. It was the kind of gaze a man gives a sample of pond scum under a microscope.

"Go," he said.

He turned to some work on his desk, pretending that Paine had already left.

After a while, Paine had.

F·I·F·T·E·E·N

T he limousine picked him up at Logan Airport. Paine had been in Boston once on police business and once when his cousin got married. Both times he'd gotten lost. Boston was a maze you drove into where, no matter how sure your sense of direction, you always arrived at a place different from your destination.

But the limo had no such problems. It glided through one-way streets like a magnet drawn to iron. The iron was Gloria Fulman.

Paine tried to look through the smoky gray glass to the front seat and see if the driver was really doing his job, or if the car worked by radio control.

There was a driver up there, because when they arrived at the Fulman Building he emerged and opened the door for Paine. Paine felt like tipping him. There was a doorman, in a smart red suit and a red pillbox hat brocaded in gold, who held the front door of the building open. Paine went in. There was a desk man, who merely nodded as Paine walked by.

He walked toward the elevator banks but a discreet cough from the desk man made him stop. The desk man smiled primly and motioned to a lone elevator set inconspicuously into the marble facade of the lobby to the left. The desk man looked down at his desk again. To him, Paine no longer existed. The man was standing. Paine wondered if he had to stand all day long.

As Paine stepped in front of the elevator, there was the audible click of a lock being disengaged. The door slid smoothly open. There was no Up button. The interior of the elevator was marble-facaded, a mock of the lobby; there were recently polished bronze columns set into the four corners, bottomed in claw feet and topped in lions' heads. The elevator ceiling was paneled in mirrors. Paine looked up at himself. He could barely feel movement, and he wondered if the elevator was moving until it bumped demurely to a stop and the door whispered open.

More marble. A hallway, the walls bordered with bronze-framed mirrors every half dozen feet. The hallway ended in a right turn. There was another length of hallway which finally ended in huge double doors. Another doorman, more red velvet and brocade. This one stood. Again no seat. The doorman had heavy-soled shoes on, brightly and blackly polished. The build underneath the pillbox cap and organ-grinder's monkey suit looked like ex-middleweight.

"Mr. Paine," the doorman said. His eyes were flat, devoid of expression.

The doorman must have been miked; he never moved but the doors opened from within. As Paine walked in, the doors were closed by yet another doorman.

This is getting silly, Paine thought.

He was in an entrance hall as large and as furnished as his apartment. Gloria Fulman was there to greet him.

"Mr. Paine," she said, her voice as flat as the doorman's.

"Hello," Paine said.

She turned, personally escorting him to a sitting room off the entrance hall. She even opened the white doors leading into it herself. Paine was more interested than flattered at the attention. She wanted more than to buy him, that was sure.

The sitting room was elegant and cold. The rugs looked as old as Persia.

"You'll take coffee?" she asked. On cue, the maid Paine had seen at the suite in New York appeared with the same silver service and the same kind of tea sandwiches. The maid handed coffee to him the way he liked it.

Gloria Fulman sat down on a lavender Sheraton sofa, and Paine sat down on a matching piece on the other side of the coffee table. As in New York, Gloria Fulman didn't touch her coffee.

"I want you to do an important piece of business for me, Mr. Paine," she said.

"And what would that be?"

"I want you to find Les Paterna's brown folder."

"You'll have to stand on line to get it."

Something stirred in the coffee-cold depths of her eyes.

"I know all about Henry Kopiak," she said. "This matter concerns the Fulmans. Your employer understands."

Paine stood up and walked to a framed etching on one wall. It was a beautifully frozen moment capturing two young girls on a swing in a park arching into the air, while a bum on a bench admired them. "So you're saying you made a deal with Barker that if I find the folder, you get it, and the hell with Kopiak?"

The etching had a pencil signature in the lower right-hand corner and was dated 1907.

Behind him, she rose from the couch.

"Mr. Paine," she said, and he turned to see her standing nearly at his elbow. She was pleasantly plump as he had remembered her, but this close he saw that she would look even more plump if she did not have the finest clothes altered with precision. If she had been forced to buy off-the-rack, she would not look so pleasant. Up close, she still looked ten years older than twenty-five.

"I'm saying that your employer expects you to do what you're paid for. My circumstances are . . . special."

He waited for her to go on. After trying to stare into his eyes for a few moments she turned and paced away from him.

"My husband," she said in a lowered, careful voice, "is in a precarious political position. There are people who will destroy him if they can."

"Are you being blackmailed?"

She stopped in front of her coffee and sat down again. She picked up the cup and then put it down. Her hand slipped, and coffee spilled over the rim onto the saucer. Paine watched a drop of it fall to the highly polished coffee table. He expected an alarm to go off, the mechanical maid to rush in with lemon polish and whisk the drop into oblivion.

Paine said, "I can smell blackmail a mile away. I smell it everywhere I look with your family." He looked at her levelly. "Did you know Lucas Druckman?"

This time he had caught her. Her eyes shifted subtly, filled in with life before going blank again. Her hand brushed across the top of her coffee cup, upsetting it again. "Who?" she said, not as firmly as she wished.

He took Druckman's picture out. "I already showed you this once."

"I don't know him," she said. She looked at the coffee table, and for a horrible moment Paine thought she was going to summon the maid to clean her spill. Instead she dabbed it up herself, with the corner of a napkin.

Paine sat down on the sofa and leaned forward. "Mrs. Fulman, has someone tried to kill you?"

"What do you mean?" she said. She was more and more unsure of herself, and Paine admitted to himself that he was enjoying it.

"I mean the bodyguards posing as bellboys you've got all over this place. I know hired muscles when I see them. This place looks like a Mafia don's love nest. I doubt you keep three armed men around all the time, even if your collection of etchings is valuable. Has someone tried to kill you?"

"Yes," she said.

"And you're sure that whoever tried to kill you killed Les Paterna, and maybe your father and sister, too?"

She had regained some of her composure. "I've hired you to find out who killed Les Paterna."

"Why do I get the feeling I'm only getting exactly what you want me to know?"

"Because that's true."

"Was Les Paterna blackmailing you?"

"That doesn't matter."

"Why didn't you tell me you knew him?"

She was silent, a part of the furniture, the room, the money itself.

Paine suddenly swept his arm across the coffee table, knocking the china cups, the coffee, the tea service, the little square sandwiches with the crusts removed, onto the rug. There were coffee droplets spattered in a line along the coffee table, and coffee stains setting comfortably into the Persian rug. He hoped they would be hard to get out. He hoped there was mayonnaise in the tea sandwiches, and that that would be hell to get out, too.

Gloria Fulman didn't move.

There was a polite knock at the double doors, and then they opened. Paine heard what sounded like a kitten crying. The maid wheeled a large white bassinet on large wheels into the room. The crying came from the bassinet.

"It's time for her four o'clock feeding, ma'am," the maid said. "I thought you'd want to know."

"Thank you, Barbara," Gloria Fulman said. There was a baby in the bassinet, small as a cat, and she picked it up. Paine studied her face and there was something akin to maternity on it.

Gloria Fulman said to Barbara, "We've had a little accident. We'll need someone to come and look at the rug. And please tell Jeff to bring the limousine around front. Mr. Paine will be going back to the airport now."

S·I·X·T·E·E·N

At twenty-five thousand feet in the air, with the sustained muffled scream of jet engines to lull him, Paine closed his eyes and the third bad place found him.

It was a night place. There was only darkness, the *snick-snick* of windshield wipers, the tarp-bright, slick blackness of wet street reflecting the colors of man-made night: dirt-yellow streetlamps, squares of dim light in rows of dead black buildings. The windows in the patrol car were down; the night smelled wet and close and dirty. Dannon was driving, and he wouldn't stop talking. He had been talking ever since they went on shift, first about his fishing trip, the Pennsylvania walleye pike he had caught in a big reservoir. Then he talked about the Yankees.

Paine felt sick. There was a constant gnaw in his belly

that had risen slowly to the back of his head and settled behind the back of his eyes where it throbbed dully. His head felt like a giant squeezed fist.

"Sure you don't want to go in?" Dannon kept asking. He knew Dannon was taunting him. Good cops did their job. Good cops stuck with their partners, didn't go in sick in the middle of a shift.

"Come on, Jack," Dannon said with mock heartiness, punching him lightly in the ribs. "Want a nice bowl of chili? Maybe a greasy bucket of Chinese ribs?"

Paine groaned and Dannon laughed.

Dannon was always like this—a sour mix of paternalism and riding, suppressed brutality. Paine had given up long ago trying to figure Dannon out. He seemed to like being a cop, but there was a deep, festering resentment in him, an itch he never scratched in front of Paine. He hovered on the edge of unpredictability. At first it had seemed like camaraderie, the complaining and dissatisfaction, but Paine had learned that Dannon's resentment also held room for Paine himself. After Paine had refused to have anything to do with Dannon's small payoffs, the free hamburgers and coffees, the twenties cheerfully collected here and there, he knew he had found his way onto Dannon's crap list.

"Little high and mighty for a rookie whose old man blew his own brother's head off, don't you think?" Dannon had said one night, his joking manner layering the hostility beneath. In the locker room he subtly rode Paine all the time, doing it in such a way that, without looking cruel, he drew laughter from anyone who was around. When they were alone, he could be just as subtle and vicious, and often was.

"Sure you don't want a taco, kid?" Dannon laughed, pushing Paine with his fist in the ribs again. His voice turned mean. "Want me to bring you in, Jack? Take you to the nurse?"

"Fuck off," Paine said.

The dull yellow lights flashing off the black wet tarp were like pins stabbing into his eyes. He wanted to squeeze his head with his hands and scream.

Dannon drove without speaking, blessing Paine with the near silence of windshield wipers slapping water from the glass in front of him.

They were in the center of Yonkers now, a run-down mix of gasping businesses and warehouses bordered by low-rent apartments. Paine fought to keep his eyes from squinting against the stabbing hurt that assaulted them from the sodium vapor lamps overhead. There had been a lot of trouble near here lately.

Dannon slowed the car to a crawl.

Paine thought his partner had seen something. Ignoring the anguish his eyes felt, he searched for a problem. If he missed something, Dannon would get on him. But there was nothing. Dannon began to talk.

"You know, kid," he said, his voice conversationally hiding the menace that crept into it, "I don't understand how you can afford to be a fucking saint."

"Let it drop," Paine said.

Dannon laughed. "I can always stop for those tacos." His tone changed to mock seriousness. "I just don't understand you."

"I told you," Paine said, wanting more than anything to ram his eyes shut, but keeping them open, looking through the sweeping path of the wipers, out through the water-spattered, half-opened window on his right, "I don't give a shit what you do. Just leave me out of it."

"You're my *partner,* Jack," Dannon went on. "I can't leave you out of anything."

"Learn."

Anger, the thing Paine had fought to control since he had started with this man, rose in him.

"Look," Dannon began, but the anger spilled over in Paine and he grabbed Dannon's arm, hard. Dannon braked the car in the middle of the street and turned his cold eyes on Paine.

"Leave me the fuck alone," Paine hissed. "I don't give a shit if you're screwing your grandmother on the side, *just leave me out.*"

Time stood still as Dannon stared into his face. Then he broke contact and turned back to the road. "All right, kid," he said quietly.

They drove in silence. The night melted away around them. Yellow lights, black streets. Yellow and black. The rain made everything ghostly; a few wisps of misty fog trailed up from the gutters to nuzzle the darkness. They circled the center of town, skirted the outskirts, started from the bottom and drove back up again.

The night stabbed at Paine and he fought to keep his eyes open.

Dannon began to say something, then stopped and said, "Holy shit."

He jerked the car to the curb and was halfway out before Paine focused on what was happening. On the sidewalk ahead of them, a man in a stylish raincoat was just collapsing to his knees. As Paine watched, he fell forward. Even in the dreamlike yellow and black light, Paine saw the red tear across the bottom of his face. And up ahead, a small figure in a leather jacket was running away.

Paine pushed his door open. Pulling his .38, Dannon ran past the fallen figure in the trench coat in pursuit of the boy in the leather jacket. He gave a quick glance back at Paine, indicating with a nod that Paine should check the fallen man.

The man in the trench coat lay unmoving, face down, next to a bench. His leather briefcase had fallen open on the ground, leaving a scatter of papers soaking in the light rain. The man was black, maybe thirty years old. He looked like he had decided to curl up and go to sleep, but he was dead.

Paine pulled him over. The left side of his neck looked like a cherry bomb had gone off in it, taking out a ragged wedge half the size of Paine's fist.

Paine settled the man back down in the rain and let him sleep forever. He looked up. Dannon was well up the street, gaining inevitably on the figure in the leather jacket. The boy took a sudden right corner and Dannon disappeared after him.

Paine ran back to the cruiser and radioed for backup. Then he followed Dannon. He reached the corner Dannon had turned, and stopped. His eyes were burning. He closed them tight and then opened them. He was surrounded by night and drizzling rain and yellow and black. He shook his head, bringing his eyes back to focus. He listened. Ahead of him footsteps slapped against wet pavement. He caught movement between two apartment buildings.

He ran. The pavement hit his feet, hard. He felt detached from himself. He felt like someone else was running, watching the pounding of feet against sidewalk. The black and yellow night blurred, cleared. He drew his hand across his eyes, pulled in burning lungfuls of air.

Dannon was twenty yards from him, motioning for Paine to follow him into an alley.

Paine stood before the opening of the alley and swayed. It looked like a cave mouth, the mouth of a dark giant beast. He stumbled forward and it swallowed him.

He fell to one knee, drew a rasping breath, then stood. His eyes focused and unfocused. He felt perhaps he should lie down in the alley, go to sleep, let the other detached self who watched him continue.

"Paine!" he heard from a great distance. It was a giant's bellow muffled by darkness, the enclosing alley, his own disjoined self.

He grunted, staggering forward.

Dannon was next to him. That much he knew. Dannon was shouting, pointing with his long hand, and Paine fought his body and stood still and looked where Dannon was pointing.

Everything slowed as if he had been dropped into water. The alley was black but suddenly it became very bright. There was light ahead. Someone stepped out of the darkness, a man-boy with a leather jacket on. He pointed something at Paine. Paine remembered the man in the trench coat with the wedge of neck missing, the thick clotting flow of red that melted into the rain and made the man sleep. The man's eyes had looked as though the life had been yanked out in one surprised pull.

"Paaaaaaaaaine!" he heard. The world slowed even more. The figure in front of Dannon's pointing finger moved, stepped into the bright light, became part of it, the thing in his hand, the bright sun-flash of the thing in his hand pointed at Paine . . .

When Paine awoke in the hospital twelve hours later Dannon was there to tell him what had happened. The boy with the leather jacket on was fifteen years old. The thing in his hand had been a four-cell Radio Shack flashlight he'd gotten for free that afternoon. He had stepped into the alley to try it out. His mother had told him not to go out but he had gone, anyway. He was not the one they were looking for. Dannon told him that he had yelled for Paine not to fire; that Paine had taken out his gun and pointed it at the boy. Dannon told him how the alley had lit up like lightning when Paine fired his .38. He hit the boy in the head from five feet away, killed him instantly.

"You yelled, 'Uncle Martin!' when you fired, Jack," Dannon said, unsmiling. Later, at the inquest, unsmiling, Dannon said the same thing.

For a while, at twenty-five thousand feet in the air, Paine imagined the jet engine's screams were his own.

S·E·V·E·N·T·E·E·N

Paine's call to Bobby Petty went right through this time. No one told him Petty was out; no one put him on hold and made him listen to bad music.

"Kicked some ass, Bobby?" Paine asked. He noticed that Petty had taken his call in the quiet place again. No typewriters, no voices.

Petty grunted.

"Dannon been bothering you?"

"Dannon can fuck himself."

"I'm sure he couldn't get it right."

"That's a cheery thought, Jack. I got you something on Lucas Druckman."

"Tell me about Druckman."

Petty hesitated. "Okay, I'll tell you about Druckman." Paine could tell there was something else Bobby had to tell him, something that he was waiting for the right moment to say.

"Is Druckman dead?" Paine asked.

"Yes, Druckman's dead. Someone found him in the trunk of a car in L.A. seven years ago with his face blown off. Somebody must have been very mad at him. LAPD figured he had sharked the wrong guy, maybe borrowed a little too much himself. Maybe he wasn't very good with records. That's not the weirdest thing about this guy, though. Looks like he was another wash job."

"Jeez . . ."

"Nobody named Lucas Druckman existed before 1970. No birth records, nothing."

"Morris Grumbach was involved with two wash jobs? Was he some sort of broker for the FBI?"

"It's possible."

"But why? And if he was, why did the FBI let the scumbags they gave him run all over him?"

"I hit a wall on that, just like with Paterna."

Paine had a sudden thought about the third photo that had been grouped with Paterna and Druckman. "Think your person in L.A. would be willing to take a look at a picture, try to make an ID?"

"Sure, drop it off," Bobby said. "He owes me a couple of favors. Listen, Jack," Bobby continued, "there's something else I've got to tell you."

"Something with Ginny? She call you or Terry?"

"Nothing like that. It's that friend of yours at the Barker Agency. Jimmy Carnaseca."

"What did Jimmy do?"

"He got killed."

"Oh, Christ Jesus."

"He was taking money from some guy to check on his

wife, and messing with her himself. The guy killed Jimmy, winged the wife." Bobby continued sarcastically, "The guy forgave the wife, says they're going to save their marriage."

"Christ," Paine said.

"I know you liked him, Jack. I'm sorry. They're going to wake him tomorrow night at Thompson's in the Bronx."

"Sure, Bobby. Listen, I've got to go."

"You'll be all right?"

Tonelessly, Paine said, "Sure."

"Like I said—"

"I'll call you if I need you, Bobby."

He let the phone fall into its cradle.

"Oh, Jesus," he said.

The night man recognized him this time and nodded briefly over the top of his *Daily News* as Paine signed in. The elevator up to the agency was noisier than usual. Paine thought of Gloria Fulman's elevator, the smooth, regularly oiled mechanism that pulled it gracefully up, the sour look that would cross Gloria Fulman's face if it dared make a noise ("Barbara, have someone look at that").

The elevator jarred to a stop and Paine yanked the rusting, lopsided gate back and pushed his way out into the lobby of the Barker Agency. The carpet was old. There was a flattened, shoe-worn tread in it that wound past Margie's reception desk and down the hall. Paine followed it to Jimmy Carnaseca's office.

"Hey, Jack, you should do what I do," he almost heard Jimmy say.

Sure, Jimmy.

The door to Jimmy's office was locked. Paine tried to push it open, and then he took off his jacket and balled it around his right fist and put it through the glass. The cheap stenciled name on the door shattered, the *J* in Jimmy falling off into darkness.

He reached in and unlocked the door. The police had been here. Nothing had been removed, but he felt like a man whose house has been entered by a stranger in his absence and, though nothing is stolen, the atmosphere itself feels violated. Everything was almost in Jimmy's place for it—Paine knew that each item had been lifted, looked over and then put back. Soon someone would come and take everything away. Whatever the police didn't want would get thrown out. Jimmy had no family. He had run away from the circus at the age of thirty to become a private eye.

Paine flipped on the light switch.

The thing Jimmy had been building was on his desk. The cops must have puzzled over that one. It was a mass of odd angles. It still looked as though it might be some sort of bridge when finished. Paine decided that that was his final guess.

Paine picked up the box. It was empty of pieces. Maybe the police had taken them. He turned the box over. There was no picture on the cover; stenciled across the blank cardboard were the words "Contents: 500 wood sticks." The box had been filled with little sticks of wood that Jimmy had randomly glued together. A practical joke.

Paine put the box down and went to Jimmy's filing cabinet. He pulled open the middle drawer. There, in the back, was the blue folder. Paine took it out and put it on the desk and sat down in front of it.

Inside the folder was a marble composition book, the kind kids buy for school. On the front cover, in the white rectangular section devoid of marbling, in florid script, was a large letter *J*.

Paine opened the book.

Pasted in the upper right-hand corner of the first page was a wallet photo. It showed a plain, middle-aged woman with a lot of wear on her face. She was smiling sadly. She looked like the kind of woman who went to mass every day and sat in the back, then went to work for someone who didn't like her very much, then went home to cook and clean for a husband who didn't like her much, either. She looked like the kind of woman who wore a kerchief when she went out.

Below the photo, in a fastidiously neat hand, was written:

At dinnertime last night Anna's husband called from Syracuse. I knew why he was in Syracuse because I followed him there on Thursday and caught him with the camera. Blonde, dumb-looking, maybe thirty-four or thirty-five. Just a little overweight. Anna didn't want to believe it but when her husband called while I was there, after I had told her, after the way he talked to her on the phone, the excuses he gave, she knew. She began to cry when she hung up the phone, and I was embarrassed, but she let me hold her.

It was still early after that, and I took her to Rye Playland and we went on some rides and I made her have her picture taken. No one had ever taken her to Rye Playland before. Her husband never takes her anywhere. I can't understand that. I finally got her to smile on the third picture in the booth and I threw the other two out. The look on her face made me want to cry.

She let me sleep with her, and I know that it was mostly for revenge against her husband, but I don't care. I think I made her feel wanted. That made me feel good.

Under that, a couple of lines down, as if it had been added later or after much thought: "For a little while I didn't feel so alone."

Paine turned the page. The next one was blank, but his thumb felt the raised imprint of another picture on the following page. He turned, and there was another sad-eyed woman, a bleached blonde with enormous amounts of eye shadow on her booze-bloated face. This one, too, was smiling, but it looked as though it was not a natural thing for her to do and might collapse at any time.

Under the picture was a similar story to the first.

Paine went slowly through the rest of the notebook. Some entries were longer than others. Some were without photographs but this meant nothing because Paine could see them in his mind's eye. They were all the same woman, really.

You should do what I do, Jack.

A footstep sounded; Paine turned in time to see Barker stop in front of the shattered fragments of Jimmy's door.

"What the hell are you doing?" Barker growled.

Paine closed the notebook and placed it on the desk.

"Did you break in here?" Barker demanded. His face was reddening and his voice rose to an unnaturally higher pitch.

"Yes."

"It comes out of your paycheck," Barker said. As he fought to bring himself under control, his voice lowered.

"That's fine," Paine said.

"I'm glad you think so. And as long as you're here now I'll tell you Gloria Fulman called me this evening. She told me about the way you acted up there and has decided to drop us. She wants us to drop the whole Grumbach case."

"We can't do that."

"Like hell we can't." He began to walk away from the doorway, stepping to avoid shards of glass, down the hall toward his office. "She's the client, Paine, and she doesn't want us anymore."

As Barker opened his office door Paine took him by the shoulder. The silk of his suit jacket felt like grease in Paine's grip.

"What about Rebecca Meyer?"

"Mrs. Fulman paid a kill fee for all the contracts. Rebecca Meyer agreed." He tried to pull away but Paine didn't let go of his shoulder.

"Don't you understand what she's doing?" Paine said. "She never had any intention of using us. This way it looks good. She hires me, gets me up there, provokes me, then fires me. And at the same time gets me away from the rest of the family."

Barker's gaze was cooly level. "You nearly ruined a five-thousand-dollar rug, which Mrs. Fulman graciously offered to forget. As for the rest, that's none of our business. Now let go of me, Paine."

"We can't drop that case."

"We already have." He tried to turn out of Paine's hold, into his office. Paine almost let him go but then he tightened his grasp on Barker's shoulder, pressing him back against the doorframe.

"You can't do that."

Alarm was rising into Barker's eyes. "Let go of me now, Paine," he said, "and I won't file assault charges." He reached with his free hand to straighten his tie. "I don't think you want to push me."

"I'll push you, asshole." Paine moved his hand from

Barker's shoulder to his back and pushed him into his office. He propelled Barker in a straight line through the maze of obstacles. The potted plant lurched over; a magazine rack was kicked to one side, spilling never-opened issues of *Architectural Digest* over the floor like a fan of cards. Barker turned to fight but Paine kept on him, shoving at his chest, and he stumbled backward.

He pushed Barker past his desk and down into the low chair on the other side of it. Sweat had broken out on Barker's face, and he had flushed into pink splotches. His tie was loosened and his handkerchief pushed out of its perfect fold in his breast pocket. His glasses were askew. His eyes had gone empty of everything but rabbitlike terror.

"You . . . wouldn't . . . dare . . ." he wheezed in a high voice.

"I might," Paine said. He loomed over Barker, then turned to the bookshelves. The hidden speakers were soothing out the Rachmaninoff Variations, a brave trill of piano answered by a muted shout from the orchestra.

"How do you turn it off?" Paine asked.

Barker was hyperventilating, breathing desperately into his cupped hands.

"Screw it," Paine said. He whisked aside unread rows of books until the tiny speakers, laid flush against the back corner walls, were revealed. He tried to dig his fingernails under the edge of the cloth grille and get them out, but they wouldn't move. Rachmaninoff mocked him, his piano questioning, orchestra answering.

"Shit!" Paine said, and then he punched his fist into the grille of the right speaker, crushing the paper cone. The left channel continued to play, piano without orchestra, and he punched it into silence also.

"You'll . . . pay for that, too," Barker panted. But his

voice was much stronger and had regained its low, arrogant tone.

Paine turned. Barker's tie was knotted tightly at his throat, his handkerchief neatly creased in his breast pocket. The red mottling had vanished into his skin like muddy water into dry ground. He had polished his glasses and straightened them on his face. He held his cigarette case open and took one out, putting it demurely to his lips.

"I might kill you yet," Paine said, but his anger was deflated by the resurrected spectacle in front of him.

"I don't think you will." Barker got up, walked deliberately past Paine to the other side of his desk. He sat in his huge leather lounge chair and swiveled it. He lit his cigarette, leaned his chair back and regarded Paine from beneath a cloud of blue-gray smoke. He pointed his right, sapphire-ringed pinky at the silent speakers.

"Thank you," he said.

He began to laugh, one of his throaty, impolite sounds that grew enormous. "God, I'm happy no one was here to see the way you made me look. I haven't looked like Manny Barkewitz in thirty years."

He laughed again, humorlessly letting it trail into his words. "I don't mind telling you, Paine. I can't see that it matters. I used to be somebody named Manny Barkewitz."

He leaned his lounger back, staring at a space somewhere near the ceiling. "My father was a sanitation worker in Brooklyn." His eyes were hard and black through cigarette smoke. "My mother took in laundry. The house always stank of it." He sniffed derisively. "I don't think I'll ever forget that smell.

"My mother and father fought every night. He'd come home, drink one beer and start yelling. His clothes smelled so bad that even the odor of starch deserted the apartment until my mother could get him to take them off so she could wash them. 'All you do is clean!' he'd yell at her. Then he'd have another beer and then another. He kept on her all night, and she'd shout right back."

He leaned toward Paine, his chair gliding forward. "And I was the prize package." He smiled. "Little Manny. Runt of the block, runt of the litter. My two sisters were big like my old man, and they made me look like the weak little shit I was. They were on me all the time." His smile grew satisfied. "One of them is dead now, the other weighs two hundred and thirty pounds. Her husband calls her a pig.

"I got beat up three times a week. The jerks in the neighborhood took turns on me. It didn't mean shit to them or anybody that I was good with numbers, or knew every batting average in the Dodger lineup. These bastards *liked* beating the shit out of me. I lost my hearing in one ear for a year because I was stupid enough to try to fight back when one of them called my mother a bitch. He proved to me she was, because she didn't do a damn thing when I told her who had beat the side of my head into steak tartare. She said she took in that kid's mother's laundry, and that we needed the money. She also said they had money and could buy lawyers.

"So, Paine," Barker said, lifting a second cigarette out of his case, then snapping the case shut loudly, slipping it back into the silk-lined pocket of his jacket, "I learned that there are two kinds of cripples in the world. There are the ones that take the shit and don't do anything about it, and are owned by somebody else, and there are the ones who stop being cripples, and own themselves. My mother died from TB a year after that kid beat me up. The doctor said she worked herself to death. I got my hearing back at her funeral."

He put his hand behind his head, tilting the lounger back. Smoke drifted up behind him. His smile was as cold as his first cigarette. "That's why I hate cripples who don't stop being cripples. Because they don't own themselves. Like you, Paine. Everybody but you owns a piece of you. I own a piece of you." He waved at his smoke. "I'm not talking about the jail sentence I could get you for assaulting me. You could handle that, probably. Maybe even your friend Petty could get you out of it. I'm talking about something else."

He angled back his chair, pulling open a small drawer in his desk. Inside was a thin machine. He lifted it out. Also in the drawer was a row of microcassettes. He looked them over briefly, then selected one. He removed a cassette from the machine and put in the one he had chosen.

"We would have been able to hear this through the speakers you destroyed. I hope the little speaker in the machine does the tape justice."

He pushed a button, and there was the hiss of rolling tape. There was a beep followed by Paine's voice saying, "What made you look for me here?" Rebecca Meyer's voice, sounding distant but clear, answered, "I called you at home. Your wife answered and said you might be here."

There was more conversation, followed by rustling sounds and panting, and then Paine heard himself say, "I have a problem there." Barker's face was filled with amusement. "That's the way," Rebecca Meyer breathed heavily a few moments later. "That's it."

There was more. Paine listened to it for a few moments and then he looked at Barker's face and Barker smiled. He turned off the machine and the sounds went away.

"There's a copy of this tape in another place," Barker said, "so please don't destroy this machine. It's very expensive and you couldn't afford to pay for it." He removed the tape and replaced it with the one that had

been in the machine. He put everything back into the
drawer and closed it.

"As you realize," Barker said, "this tape is useless to me
as far as you are concerned. But it could do consider-
able damage to Rebecca Meyer. She's in the middle of a
rather delicate divorce at the moment. Her husband, Gerald, and his many lawyers would love to get hold of
this."

"You and Gloria Fulman used it as a lever on Rebecca to
get her to drop the case."

Barker shrugged. "Let's say they had a sisterly chat over
the telephone." He plucked a third cigarette from his case,
looked down at it. "You're fired, of course. I'd like you to
leave immediately."

Paine thought about hitting him. He thought about
hitting him until his teeth slid out of their gums and his
mouth was full of blood. He thought about hitting him
until that ugly crippled loser little-boy look came back into
his eyes. He wanted to see Manny Barkewitz, the proto-
Barker, the scared, bitter human mold that had made the
less-than-human thing in front of him. If he did that, if he
made Barker see that he was still the scared bitter little boy
that everybody beat up on, that nothing had changed, that
for all his faking, all his makeup and careful tailoring and
false practiced looks, he was still a cripple, then perhaps
Barker would truly own himself. Perhaps if he saw that we
are all cripples, and that we all get beat up, and badly, and
that ultimately the bully who does the beating isn't the fat
kid with pimples who lives on the next block, or the tall kid
with thin blond hair over his collar and a $1.98 switch-
blade out to impress his friends because he can't impress
himself, but the cold night itself, perhaps then he could
truly put Manny Barkewitz to rest.

Instead of teaching a valuable lesson, Paine said, "Good-bye, Barker."

In his apartment Paine dialed the phone. It rang for a long time and then Gerald Meyer answered it. He sounded as though he had been in Morris Grumbach's dark green study, using the bar.

"Dear Rebecca left for parts unknown," he said brightly. "She packed and went. Didn't leave any note for you, dear boy."

Paine interrupted the monologue. "Do you have any idea where she might have gone?"

He laughed. "Lord, no. She may have gone to Cape Cod, possibly to Maine, maybe even to Nova Scotia. The wonderful Grumbachs have homes everywhere. Perhaps she went to London, or Switzerland. I'm sure she'll be back before too long. Any message, old fellow?"

Paine hung up.

He dialed another number. Bob Petty was groggy when he answered.

"Beauty sleep, Bob?" Paine asked.

Petty forced himself into wakefulness. "Fell asleep in front of the TV. *Hill Street Blues.* Lousy show." He yawned.

"Get anything on that picture?" Paine asked.

"Christ, I only faxed it out to L.A. a couple of hours ago," Petty complained. "Actually, I tried to reach you before I fell asleep. I got a call back on it just as I was leaving work. Hold on."

Petty went away from the phone; Paine heard the mumble of a television set abruptly cut to silence and then a barely audible exchange of words. The other voice sounded like Terry's. Petty uttered a curse that Paine heard clearly. Both voices receded. Finally, Petty returned to the phone.

"Sorry about that, Jack. Terry almost washed my shirt with your information in the pocket." Paine heard the crackle of paper. "They found your bird right away. His name was Jeffrey Steppen."

"Was?"

"Naturally. Died in 1970. At least this one had a birth date, though. Born in 1935."

"How did he die?"

"Fell off a boat and drowned, north of L.A. Body was never recovered. Are you ready? Morris Grumbach owned the boat."

"Wow."

"Yeah, and it stays interesting. Steppen was an FBI agent."

"Jesus. There's our FBI connection."

"My buddy Ray is trying to find out what he can about Steppen, but don't expect much. The FBI is tight on their own people."

"Can't thank you enough, Bobby."

"Getting real interesting, Jack."

Paine hung up and dialed the California number on the slip of paper in his wallet. The woman who had been yelling at Izzy said, "Hello?" Paine hung up the phone.

He took out the packets of photos and went through them until he found the one with the man and woman and horse. A stand of eucalyptus trees bordered the field to the left.

Paine put the picture away and began to pack.

E·I·G·H·T·E·E·N

This wasn't Boston, and Paine wasn't in a limousine. Driving a rented Escort, he saw more of L.A. than he needed. Any of it, he decided, was too much. It looked like every lousy television show portrayed it: wide-open spaces filled with a multitude of facades. It looked like it had been glued together haphazardly, like Jimmy Carnaseca's practical joke. Even the sky was a facade: so wide and blue it hurt his eyes, but, when viewed from the hills above the city, revealing itself as an orange cumulus that had hurt his eyes not with its breadth, but with its sulphur dioxide content. He had been in Tucson once, a place that was supposed to be good for your lungs; but, forty miles beyond the city, from the summit of Kitt Peak where he'd gone to see the telescopes perched on that sacred mountain like God's eyes, he'd been startled to see a similar salmon-colored cloud hanging over that

Arizona town. Los Angeles (there were *fallen* angels, weren't there?) made Tucson's smog look like fresh air. He doubted if you could see any stars—never mind the Big Dipper—from the center of L.A.

The place he was looking for turned out not to be the seedbag apartment he'd imagined, but a tidy ranch house at the edge of the Hollywood Hills. It might even show on some outdated celebrity map, labeled the home of a rising television star.

The house had had security, at one time. There were bolt marks bereft of paint on the chin-high wrought-iron fence where the cameras had been, and the heavy iron gate showed a sawed-out spot where a remote lock had been. The television star had moved, and the new tenants hadn't kept up the payments on the security system.

Paine pushed the gate open and walked a path through a tiny garden of unwatered flowers to the front door.

The woman opened it, and she had the phoniest smile he'd ever seen. "Oh?" she said perkily, striking an artless pose. She looked like a cheap model fondling an auto show Buick. He had imagined her fat and blonde, but she was anorexic and her hair was long and red. She was about fifty-five, the might-as-well-be-dead age for women on the make in California. She looked vaguely familiar— someone who might have played an aging actress looking for an aging mate on *The Love Boat.*

"Let me see Izzy," Paine said.

He saw Izzy, behind the redhead, just reaching the bottom of the stairs. It looked like she had found her aging mate.

She said, "You're not from Max Dugan's Agency—" and then she stopped. She tried to close the door on him but he put his arm against it and pushed his way in. She almost fell. He closed the door behind him and helped the redhead balance herself. He walked her toward the kitchen, where Izzy was moving around, pulling drawers open.

When he got to the open doorway of the kitchen he pushed the woman in ahead of him. He had expected Izzy to come at him with something substantial but he had only a steak knife and he was backed against the open drawer he'd pulled it out of. As Paine entered the room, Izzy tensed back, sliding the drawer closed with his butt.

"Get the fuck away," Izzy stammered.

He was closer to the way Paine had imagined him than the woman was, runty, balding, but where Paine's imagination had stopped he was also tanned, and dressed in a silk robe with a Spandex brief swimsuit underneath. There were three or four gold chains around his neck.

"Goddammit, Izzy!" the redhead yelled. She was both accusing and cheering him on. *"Goddammit!"*

She backed toward Izzy, who hadn't moved, and she grabbed the steak knife from him and went toward Paine. He waited patiently for her. She came at him with the knife overhead like any good movie psycho, but she knew more than Paine had counted on and at the last moment she brought the knife down in a roundhouse and barely missed his side. He threw his arm out and met her at the elbow, but she proved even better, and instead of the force of contact knocking the knife from her hand, she moved with his blow and brought her wrist back and then toward him. This time she drew a thin serrated cut through the top of his knuckles. It was time to take her seriously. He kicked her feet out from under her and stepped on her wrist, pressing down to make her drop the knife. She didn't. She held on to it and curled it up at his ankle, cutting him again. Paine put all his weight on her wrist, and her hand began to turn purple and she let go of the steak knife. Paine kicked it away. He had a good idea what she would try next, so he bent down and punched her smartly in the mouth before she could get her teeth on him. She quit, then.

"Jesus, why did you do that!" she screeched, rolling over on the floor, continuing to whine through the sore hand she held to her bleeding mouth.

"I'll do it again if you don't shut up."

"Christ! How can I work like this?"

Izzy found his legs and tried to run past Paine, who easily blocked his way.

"Let's talk," Paine said, putting the flat of his hand on Izzy's chest and pinning him against the wall.

"Jesus, man, don't hurt me," Izzy begged. He looked at the redhead on the floor. "Don't do anything to me."

"We'll see," Paine said.

"Jesus," Izzy said. His hands clutched protectively at the front of his robe.

Paine removed his hand from Izzy's chest and drew out the note from Les Paterna's office. He handed it to Izzy.

Izzy gave the same intake of breath he had on the phone. In person it was more dramatic. His eyes rolled back for an instant. He looked at Paine; something he thought he saw on Paine's face made him loose in the knees and he buckled to the floor and began to plead in earnest.

"Oh, Jesus, I'll get you the money. If that's what you want I'll get the thirty-three grand. That bastard Paterna. That bastard. He sold it to you, didn't he? That stinking bastard." He was wringing his hands, and now he turned on the woman on the floor. "I told you we couldn't trust the bastard, didn't I? Sooner or later, didn't I tell you that? Didn't I say the first time he got into trouble he'd sell that note? Didn't I tell you not to trust him when he didn't give it back to us?" He motioned a kick at her and turned to Paine.

"Jesus, please. I'll give it all to you next week. The whole thirty-three. Mona's got work coming the end of this week, I've got something at Universal on Monday—I swear it. Jesus, just don't blow me away."

"What about her?" Paine asked.

He looked at Mona, who was sitting up, eyeing Izzy with a kind of awe.

"Jesus, kill her, fuck her, do whatever you want. I'll get you the money, just don't hurt me."

"Shut up," Paine said to Izzy.

"Oh, God, oh, Jesus, just tell me we can talk, say you won't blow me away before we talk."

"Shut up."

"Oh, Jesus, Jesus."

Izzy moaned, holding his head in his hands.

Paine pulled out a kitchen chair from the table and said to Izzy, "Sit down."

"Oh, God, oh, Jesus."

Izzy did as he was told. As he passed Mona, she grabbed his leg and sunk her teeth into the calf. Izzy gave a womanly scream and threw his hands into the air, falling across the kitchen table with Mona's mouth still attached to the back of his shin.

Paine kicked Mona and she let go of Izzy, cursing him through her broken lip. "Motherfucker. Tell him to kill me, fuck me." The tear in her lip made her wince. She lowered her invective to a mumble. "I'll fuck *you,* you shit."

"Oh, God!" Izzy sat bent over his middle, clutching the back of his bleeding leg.

"What do you do—TV comedy?" Paine asked, gaining a sullen stare from Mona and a reprieve in Izzy's self-absorption.

"Answer me carefully," Paine said. He made himself

sound like somebody who had, in fact, come there to blow their fucking heads off.

"Anything you want," Izzy grimaced. *"Anything—"*

"Motherfucker—" Mona spat at him.

Paine took out the photos of Paterna, Druckman and Steppen and handed them to Izzy.

If anything, Izzy's intake of breath was even more dramatic this time. "You've got all three." He looked more puzzled than alarmed. "I don't get it. Did he send you?" He handed the photos to Mona.

"He's not here to do us," Mona immediately snapped at Izzy.

A light came into Izzy's eyes. "Let me see your piece." The fear in his voice was gone.

Paine did nothing.

Nursing the back of his leg, Izzy practiced a tiny smile. "Let's see it, big shot."

"I don't have a gun," Paine said. "I'm going to do you with my bare hands."

"Magnum, P.I.!" Izzy cried triumphantly. He stood, winced with pain and sat down holding his leg. *"Magnum, P.I.*—that was the show!" He snapped a finger. "There was another script they called me in on, last-minute job. Setup just like this. Guy coming in from the side, doing a little free blackmail by giving another guy his own note to collect on." He looked up at Paine. "Paterna sent you, right?"

"Paterna's dead."

Confusion filled Izzy's face. "Then maybe you found the note, figure a little action for yourself—"

"Shut up, Izzy," Mona said. She was eyeing Paine like a falcon. "This guy's a jerk. He doesn't know anything."

Paine took out the second packet of photographs and handed it to Izzy. The result was the normal dose of surprise. Izzy handed them to Mona and said, "For some-body who knows nothing, he's got plenty."

"I told you to shut up, Izzy." She handed everything back to Paine. "Get out," she said.

"Now wait, Mona," Izzy said. "If Paterna's dead, maybe we should find out—"

"Fuck you, Izzy." Her sharp eyes stayed on Paine. "He's a P.I. and he knows nothing." She stood finally and put on the bad-actress smile she had greeted Paine with at the doorway. "Good-bye," she said, waving her hand theatri-cally at the front hallway.

Paine shrugged and began to walk toward the front. "Fine," he said. "If it means anything to you, at least three people have already been murdered in this mess, including Les Paterna." He took one of his cards out of his pocket and tossed it on the floor. "I'm getting out of this lousy town of yours and going back to New York. You're on your own. You were afraid enough of dying ten minutes ago, but if you want to be brave now, be my guest."

He looked at Izzy, who had taken his cue from Mona and smiled happily. "Bye-bye, P.I.," he said.

He was getting his boarding pass when he was paged over the loudspeaker system.

He took the courtesy phone and Izzy said, "Paine?"

"Change your mind?"

"Maybe." In the background, Mona was yattering at him as usual; finally Izzy just yelled, "Shut up!" and came back on the line.

"I'm thinking maybe we can deal." Paine imagined him fingering his gold chains over his blue bikini swim trunks. "I'm thinking—"

Mona's voice sounded, close by, and Izzy yelled at her.

"Give me the phone, motherfucker!" she shouted.

"Get away, bitch!" Izzy told Paine to hold on and the fight continued until Mona began to scream, "You opened up my lip again, motherfucker! *How am I going to work?"*

"Sorry," Izzy said into the phone. "I give you something, you give me something, Paine. Here's yours: Paterna, Druckman, Steppen, all the same man. Now tell me: you sure Paterna's dead?"

"Is that what you want?"

Silence on the other end.

"Paterna's dead. Somebody hung him a couple of days ago, made it look like suicide."

"He called me a week ago, said someone had threatened to kill him."

"You thought that's who I was?"

"Yeah."

"Did Paterna call you after Morris Grumbach committed suicide?"

"Grumbach didn't kill himself. Whoever called Paterna told him he'd killed Grumbach."

"Do you have any idea who it was?"

"You give me one, Paine. Know any cops in New York or L.A. you trust?"

Paine thought of Petty's friend Ray. "One on each end."

"You sure? This is nasty stuff we're talking about here. I've been living on this for twenty-five years."

"I can take care of you."

"Come and talk."

Paine started to answer, but the phone went out. He called the number back, but no one answered. The last thing he had heard was Mona calling Izzy bad names in the background.

The car ride was even less pleasant the second time. The sky had turned from high phony blue to low, angry clouds.

It was sticky and hot. Paine's jacket stuck to his arms. The back of his neck felt like smog had pooled there. To his left, somewhere, was the big ocean that washed California, sought to purify it, but he didn't have the time to let it wash him clean.

The first drops of smog-laden rain spattered his windshield as he topped the hill within sight of the house. He braked where he was and pulled inconspicuously to the curb. Three LAPD cruisers and an ambulance were parked at various angles around the front. The first had done a movie brake job, leaving tire marks on the street and fishtailing till the front of the car pointed at the gate. The others had performed less perfect versions of the maneuver. A news crew was out of its van, its lights making an angry, rainy afternoon into bright daylight as two body bags were carried from the house over the sad trampled garden and into the tomb doors at the back of the ambulance. Following the body bags, fully aware of his moment of television immortality, strutted a plainclothesman bearing two clear-plastic bags filled with coils of rope crudely noosed at the ends.

"Shit," Paine said.

Inconspicuously, he backed the car down the hill and drove back to the airport.

N·I·N·E·T·E·E·N

The bags filled with Ginny's clothes were back on the chair.

He went into the apartment. He heard her in the kitchen, moving things around; she came out into the living room and blinked at him and said, "Hello, Jack."

It was not the same way she had said, "Good-bye, Jack."

She had a mug of coffee in her hand, and she became aware of it. She began to sip from it, changed her mind and lowered it.

"I just made some," she said, not looking at him, indicating the kitchen with her free hand.

"Your little deal fall apart?"

She looked down at the mug of coffee, and then she raised her eyes and looked at him directly. She was trying to be defiant, but it wasn't working and she knew it.

"We started fighting by the time we got to Roger's place in Montauk," she said. "He . . ."

"It was *his* fault?" Paine said, a sarcastic edge in his voice.

"We . . . fought. Look, Jack. I came back because I've thought about a lot of things and—"

"Forget it, Ginny."

"I thought about us really trying to make it work. If the two of us just give in—"

"We've been through this. Forget it."

Now she was defiant. "Goddammit, Jack, what do you want me to say?"

"I've thought a lot about this, too, and I want you to finally admit to yourself that you don't love me." She started to protest but he continued through it. "You've never loved me, Ginny. That's the problem, it's always been the problem." He singled each word out. *"You don't love me.* You've never been able to admit that to yourself. You always thought that if you messed with me a little more, changed me around a little more, that I'd be what you wanted. You've never looked at me and said, 'Here's Jack Paine, he's really fucked up, but I love him.' I never tried to change you, Ginny. I saw you that first time, and I fell in love with you, and that was it. I took *you,* Ginny, but you never took me."

There were things she was going to say. She ran through her gamut of expressions, from anger to denunciation, ending on the verge of tears.

"It's done, Ginny," he said to her quietly.

She stood with the coffee mug in her hand, and Paine wanted, as badly as he had wanted to put the gun to his head or the bottle to his lips the night before, to go to her and put his arms around her and say, "Yes." He wanted to say, "I still love you, and I'll try to change, I'll try not to be fucked up anymore and we'll try to make it work." But he knew what would happen if he did that. Someday he would see that frozen look on her face again, the one that said, "Go ahead, pull the trigger, get it over with," and he would pull the trigger for her. Finally, he would have changed for her, and he would no longer be her failure and she would be rid of him because she would possess him in the way she had always desired, which was to possess him so that he no longer possessed himself. She would own, not a piece of him as Barker did, but, in the end, all of him.

"Please go, Ginny," he said, and she stood a moment more and then she put the mug of coffee down and walked to the bags of clothes and gathered them up in her arms and opened the door and was gone. Paine heard the elevator work, but this time it was not leaving to take her away from him. It was simply leaving.

He walked to where she had put her coffee mug, and as he picked it up some of the coffee spilled out onto the carpet. He thought of Gloria Fulman and her Persian rug.

He went to the kitchen, and he poured the coffee into the drain, watching it spiral down to the depths of the earth, and said, "Good-bye, Ginny."

He showered California off his body, then dressed in a suit and tie and went to his car.

He drove to the Bronx in the dark. No stars to look at through the windshield tonight; a little of that low, angry, hot weather had followed him across the country. The back of his neck was pooled with sweat again. Muggy was muggy.

There was a white car far back that might be pacing him. He slowed, trying to lure it past, but it stayed stubbornly back. On the Major Deegan Expressway it disappeared from his rearview mirror, but when he got off he spotted it again, mounting the off-ramp as he turned onto Fordham Road at the top. The car was a BMW or Mercedes.

He waited ten minutes in the shadow of a White Castle hamburger joint, but it didn't pass. Then he pulled out conspicuously, hoping to flush it out. It was gone.

Thompson's Funeral Home was only two blocks from the Bronx Zoo. Paine pulled into the driveway, past the sign. The signs on funeral homes are all the same, bright white bordered in black. You don't have to read the name to know where you are.

The parking lot in back was big for the Bronx. He pulled into a spot bounded by bushes that had no cars to either side of it. He got out, straightened his suit and went in.

A young man with a sad face and hands folded permanently in front of him dispatched him solemnly in the right direction. He walked into a crowded room. There were a lot of high school students, some weeping onto each other; the rest were adults clustered to one side in shocked groups of three or four. The casket was closed. Paine looked at the name on the white-lettered sign at the entrance and discovered that he had walked into the wrong chapel. Closed casket. Teenager, probably; car collision, through the windshield.

He found Jimmy's chapel next door, and it was what he had expected. Small room, low lighting, taped organ music. The air smelled like refrigerant. The casket was open, and even from the doorway he could see Jimmy propped unnaturally high, compensation for his shortness. The chapel was empty.

Paine walked on the red plush carpeting and listened to the organ music. Just audible, like Rachmaninoff in Barker's office. Muted weeping filtered in from the auto death next door.

There was a kneeler before the casket. Paine stood. Jimmy's eyes were paraffined closed. His head was tilted to the left; one of the slugs had caught him just above the ear on that side and the boys in the cellar had done what they could. It wasn't all that great. Jimmy looked like waxed fruit.

"So long, Jimmy," Paine said, and with the common trick of anticipation, Jimmy's resin smile seemed to widen.

Paine left the empty room. A couple in dress and suit passed him, holding each other up; they entered Jimmy's chapel, realized their mistake and backtracked to the automobile accident next door. Organ music soothed. The ventriloquist dummy with the folded hands bowed his head at Paine as he passed.

"Good evening, sir."

"Sure," Paine said, and went into the night.

There were two of them, and they had waited for him in the stand of bushes in front of his car. It was easy for them. They stepped out as he put his key in the lock; he heard them but when he looked up there was an arm in front of his face and that was the last thing he saw. One of them hit him in the face to get him to cover up, and then the other one pumped blows to his belly and groin. Paine heard a grating laugh. They worked on him methodically, and when he was finally down they kicked him toward unconsciousness. Just before he went there, he felt a burning explosion in his groin and heard one of them say, "Hit *me* in the hangers?"

Lights passed overhead. He thought someone was shining a light in his eyes, flashing it back and forth. He reached up his arm to push away the flashlight. His arm hurt, and he couldn't raise it up. *"Stop,"* he tried to say, but his mouth didn't work well, either. It tasted like it was filled with bloody sponges.

He closed his eyes, and when he opened them again the lights were still flashing. But his eyes worked better now. They focused for him. The flashing lights were streetlamps, passing overhead. He was staring through the back windshield of a car. It was clean, and had defogger wires embedded in it. He tried to look closer at the defogger wires but his eyes unfocused again, and his body told him to return to unconsciousness.

When he opened his eyes this time, they stayed focused. The streetlights were gone. Up through the windshield was crisp dark sky. He recognized a turn of diamond stars shaped vaguely like a *W*. The constellation Cassiopeia.

Someone opened the car door.

The night that came into the car was as cool and dark as it looked through the windshield.

He expected rough hands to pull him out of the car onto the pavement, but instead, a head stared upside down into his face, and kissed him.

"You're alive." Rebecca Meyer smiled.

"Yes," his mouth tried to say, without success.

"Can you sit up?" she asked. She put her hands under his arms and pulled, but he must have cried out because she took her hands back. He tried to sit up. The world wheeled and his eyes threatened to unfocus but he made it to a sitting position and rested his head on the back of the seat. She sat next to him.

"How did you find me?" he asked thickly.

"Bob Petty said you'd be at your friend's wake. I found you in a pool of your own blood. I thought you were dead."

"I am."

He looked into her brown turbid eyes that he already knew so well. He was very tired. She was speaking slowly, but he couldn't hear her. He looked at her mouth, and it looked like she said, "Oh, shit," and, as the blurry world of unconsciousness claimed him yet again, he was sure he fell into her arms.

T·W·E·N·T·Y

His body was not young anymore.

He had taken worse beatings, but this time his body did not let him heal easily. Perhaps his mind was healing, too, letting the world spin while accountings were made, checks and balances restored. He felt like a drained bottle, not only empty, but not even knowing what he had been filled with to start.

He awoke the first morning in a bed facing the largest picture window he had ever seen. The night cold he had felt had not been an illusion; there was a sprinkling of early white snow on the leveled lawns down to the tennis court and, beyond that, the Hudson River was bathed in autumn fog.

The house itself was not cold. The fireplace in the second-floor bedroom he occupied filled half of one stone wall. Above the fireplace was the proud antlered head of an elk. The opposite wall was dominated by a Turner oil flanked by the heads of a cheetah and black leopard.

Paine tried to move and nothing happened. His body felt as real as that of the elk over the fireplace. Bandages shifted under the covers.

The morning passed. He watched the fog evaporate over the Hudson, and the tenuous dusting of white snow turn back to green lawn. He watched the gardener inspect the trellises along the path to the tennis courts for frost damage.

She came to him when the sun was high over the river. She sat on the end of the bed and looked at him for a long while. Her hair looked longer, brushed back over her eyes.

"I'm in love with you," he said.

"I know," she said.

She lay her head on him, on a place where it didn't hurt. Outside, the world turned from summer to autumn.

The next day he felt better. Four of his ribs had been taped. He still felt like a punching bag after a workout, but he sat up and looked through the window as rain fell on Westchester. In the afternoon the clouds cleared out and the sun burned through. It was in the 70s by late afternoon. He watched Rebecca and Gerald play tennis. As the sun went down he brought the telephone from the nightstand onto the bed and dialed it.

"Bobby?"

"Where the hell are you, Jack?"

"Somewhere. What's going on?"

"I have a warrant for your arrest. Were you in California two days ago?"

"I was in California. I put my fingerprints all over that

house and left my card. Then someone came in and hung the two of them."

"Great. Should we extradite you to California or would you rather go on trial in New York first?"

"Isn't murdering two California creeps more serious than beating up one former employer?"

"Not if your former employer is owed by the police commissioner. Barker wants your balls in a paper cup."

"Can you handle him?"

"I can try."

"Great. Anything from your friend on Steppen and the FBI? I found out that Steppen, Druckman and Paterna were all the same creep."

Bobby whistled. "It makes sense. Ray found that Steppen was a paperboy for the FBI—he could get any kind of document you wanted. He was involved in witness relocation but he was pretty much a rotten apple from the beginning. Got into a couple of jams early in his career, mixed up with loan-sharking, but he was good and they needed him, so they kept him around as a free-lance. Finally they just kicked him out in 1968."

"That explains how he turned from Steppen into Druckman into Paterna, but it doesn't explain why. Or what he had to do with Morris Grumbach."

Petty sighed. "Where are you, Jack?"

"Can't tell you."

"Dannon's really heating things up here over you. And the way things are now, nobody would mind if you came in DOA."

"Fine."

"Come in and talk, Jack. It might be the only way I can protect you."

"Talk to you soon, Bobby."

"Jack—"

Paine hung up the phone.

"Can't tell you where I am, Bobby."

They had dinner in Paine's room, by light from the table lamp next to the bed. Outside, there was blackness interrupted periodically by the red and green blinking lights of an airplane passing up the river. There weren't even drapes to hide the picture window at night.

"This was my father's bedroom," Rebecca said. "My sisters and I used to play in here when we were little, when my father was away. We made believe the animals on the wall were real and might leap out at us any minute."

"Where did your father get the animals?" Paine asked.

"Oh, he was a hunter when he was younger. He knew Hemingway, went on safari with him once or twice. My father knew a lot of people. You never saw his name in the paper, but he was always near power."

"Did your mother and father always have separate bedrooms?"

His question drew her back from memory. "Oh, yes. Always. My mother's bedroom is down the hall. It's all in blue and silver. No picture windows there. Everything is closed tight against the world."

There was wine on the tray which lay on the bed, and she filled their glasses.

"What about you, Jack?" she asked. "Do you have painful memories?"

"Are we talking about painful memories?"

"All memories are painful." She smiled distractedly. She seemed to take more solace in the darkness outside the window than in his face. "Now I think they all are."

Yet again, Paine almost knew why she affected him so strongly; why he was so drawn to her. And yet again, the reasons danced away and fell beyond him.

"Tell me your most painful memory," she said abruptly, turning from the dark window to look at him and pin him with her eyes.

And then, suddenly, he wanted to tell her what he had never told anyone.

"I've never dreamed about it," he said. "I've dreamed about other things but never this."

She looked into him, over the rim of her wineglass, red liquid sliding back and forth in the glass like blood, like waves against the dark banks of the Hudson.

And then he told her.

It was a Saturday afternoon. His father had to work an extra shift, so his Uncle Martin volunteered to pick him up after his Little League game. His father hesitated, but finally said yes.

His uncle came about the fourth inning and sat in the stands and watched. Jack got two hits that day, a double and a triple that was almost a home run. He was thrown out at the plate. It was a good game, and he felt good because it was summer and he didn't have to work mowing lawns for another two weeks and there were still two ball games between now and then. The sun was out every day. It was warm, but he never felt the heat; it rolled off him and into the green grass.

His uncle watched the game, and Jack looked over every once in a while to make sure he was enjoying it. He was sitting quietly in the stands, with a fisherman's hat pushed back on his head, his elbows splayed out on the bench to either side of him. He sat in the upper tier, in a corner where no one else was.

Jack didn't know much about his uncle; he'd been around, off and on, and once he'd bought him a windup boat—a huge thing with a good slow-working spring in the mother that he and his brother, Tom, used on the artificial lake in the park. Another time he brought both Jack and Tom books about space. But Jack hadn't really seen him that much, and he and his father didn't seem to be all that close. His uncle had been in the Army for a long time, in the war and then overseas in Germany. He was an M.P. His father used to talk about him every once in a while as his big brother, but there was about six years' difference between them and it seemed like they never got to know each other very well.

So his uncle watched the game, smiling or squinting against the sun. Jack couldn't tell which.

After the game was over, after Jack's team won and gathered in a circle and threw their hats into the air, his uncle stood at the bottom of the grandstand with his hands in the pockets of his bright blue jacket and he smiled. He put his arm around Jack and said, "How you been, kiddo?"

They got in his car, and Uncle Martin talked about getting something to eat. Jack said he thought they should go back to the house; he was supposed to meet Tom there to play some more ball in the backyard.

His uncle looked over at him and smiled. "I'll get you back before you know it, kiddo."

He kept driving. They drove for a long time. His uncle kept making excuses for why they weren't going to Jack's house. "We'll get there soon," he said.

They drove about an hour outside the city, then they stopped at a hamburger place. They sat outside and ate on one of the round white enameled-metal tables. Uncle Martin spread a map out and began to study it. He pushed his fisherman's hat farther back and scratched his head. "No," he said, once or twice. Then he said, "That's it."

"What's it?" Jack asked.

Uncle Martin folded the map and smiled. "A surprise,"

he said. "Your father didn't want me to tell you till we got there."

Jack stared at him, and Uncle Martin gave a hearty laugh and reached across the table and slapped Jack's shoulder. "I'm taking you on a trip!"

Jack regarded him blankly. "What do you mean?"

"We're going to go someplace, you and I."

"But what about my father and Tom?" Jack protested. "I don't have any clothes."

"Your dad said it was fine. Said you needed a treat after the school year you put in. Where we're going there are clothes and everything. Do you like to fish?"

Through his perplexity, Jack's eyes brightened.

"That's right, kiddo—we're going to fish, and camp out, we're going to do all kinds of things. You know," he said, "I've been waiting a long time for this. Did your father ever tell you what a good fisherman I was?"

He searched his memory and found nothing, but his uncle had such an earnest, expectant look on his face that he nodded. "Yes."

"He did?" Uncle Martin said. His face lit up. "Well, I'll be damned."

Uncle Martin became thoughtful again, and suddenly he got up and cleared the table and said they should be going. "Got a long ride ahead of us," he said.

They got into the car and Uncle Martin reached under the driver's seat and took out an open pair of handcuffs. "Darn seat belt doesn't work very well, kiddo," he explained, snapping one of the cuffs around Jack's right wrist and the other to the door handle. He did it so quickly and solemnly that Jack didn't question it. "I believe in safety," Uncle Martin said, and then he started the car.

They ate up a lot of highway. They crossed New Jersey

into Pennsylvania. Jack slept for a while. When he awoke they were in the Poconos. His uncle was humming to the radio, which was tuned to a station playing 101 Strings. Jack's wrist hurt where the cuff had tightened into it. His uncle saw him try to loosen it and reached over and pulled his left hand away.

"Leave it be," he said seriously. "Safety, like I said."

They drove up into the Poconos, through and beyond the summer communities, into an area as lonely as Eden. Macadam turned to dirt, then to trail. Then without warning the car found a short flat driveway that curved to a dead stop in front of a cabin. It looked like any other vacation home, with a short deck out front.

Uncle Martin got out of the car and jogged around to Jack's side. He opened the door, deftly unlocked the cuff from the door handle and pulled Jack out of the car by it. Jack yelped a protest, but Uncle Martin ignored him, still humming. Now, suddenly, Jack was afraid, and started to resist the cuffs, but Uncle Martin only turned to him and told him to be quiet. "The fishing tackle is inside," he said.

Uncle Martin brought him into the house, through a big living room with a huge stone fireplace and attached kitchen, and up the stairs. There were two closed doors off the stairway, and Uncle Martin opened the first one.

There was balloon wallpaper on the walls. A brand-new Sears bed butted one wall, with a rodeo pattern coverlet turned down. The sheets had Roy Rogers's face on them, with Trigger's profile next to him from the neck up. Roy smiled wryly, like he always did, eyes squinting. There was a new Sears chest of drawers, too, the tag still on it; on top of it was a hand mirror, an ebony-handled hairbrush, an old coin bank in the shape of a baseball made out of printed tin. The closet was open, filled with new jeans, shirts and a blue suit. There were pajamas and white shirts and socks still in their bags, the shirts folded around flat pieces of cardboard to keep them stiff, with pins stuck in the collar to keep them in place.

"This is your room," Uncle Martin said quietly, pulling Jack gently in by the cuffs. Behind the door was a long package wrapped in brown paper. Uncle Martin picked it up and handed it to Jack.

"Open it," he said.

Jack opened it. There was fishing tackle in it, a pole, a freshwater lightweight reel spooled with four-pound test line, a clear-plastic tray of panfish lures and red and white bobbers and split-shot sinkers.

"I didn't lie," Uncle Martin said.

Jack stood in the middle of the room, and he began to cry. Tears rolled out of him and he couldn't stop. The fishing pole fell out of his hand to the floor.

His uncle stood nervously next to him, holding the open end of the handcuffs, and then he said quietly, "I'll leave you now," and he dropped the cuffs and left the room and bolted the door behind him.

It was then that Jack saw that there were no windows in the room.

They fished three or four times a week. There were trout streams nearby, and a small lake a quarter mile beyond that. His uncle got him up at six in the morning, made breakfast, sometimes waffles and bacon, and then they dressed and fished. For the first two weeks his uncle told him that this was what his father wanted, but after that he said nothing.

Jack tried to get away the first day they went fishing, but his uncle tracked him down in under an hour and brought him back. A week later he tried again, but his uncle found him in thirty minutes. He didn't try again for a while. He asked small questions here and there, and discovered that his uncle owned five square miles of land. The nearest neighbor was eight miles away to the west.

Sometimes his uncle called him Jerry, his father's name.

Days went by, and weeks, and months. When his uncle went out without him he cuffed Jack to a ring anchored in the stone mantel over the fireplace. His uncle hunted a few times, bringing down a stag deer in late August. His uncle skinned and butchered it. He packed all but two steaks in the freezer, and that night Jack had venison for the first time. Also that night the weather turned cooler.

He hadn't tried to run away since June. He continued to ask small questions.

One day in mid-September his uncle went into town for supplies, cuffing Jack to the ring in the mantel. Jack had patiently worked on the ring for three months. As his uncle's truck pulled away he slipped the ring out of the wall.

Under his bed, he had squirreled a full three days' provisions into a canvas sack. The sack had two strips of heavy cloth sewn to it, making a crude backpack. Jack put it on and went to his uncle's bedroom where he hoped to find one of his uncle's rifles.

He'd never been in this room. "Now, Jerry," his uncle had told him, "I want you to stay out of my room. It's all I've got." There was a dead-bolt lock on the door. Jack tried the knob. It was locked. He threw himself against it. The first time the wood yielded slightly, but held the lock; the second time, the bolt splintered and the door flew inward.

The room was dark. No windows in here, either. Jack felt

around for a wall switch but couldn't locate one. Then he saw a pull chain hanging from the ceiling in the center of the room.

He groped for it, found it, pulled the chain.

The light went on in the room.

A chill shot through him.

The room was almost antiseptically empty. There was an army cot, crisply made, against one wall, and nothing else. The cot had white top and bottom sheets and a gray wool camp blanket. The floor was bare, unvarnished wood. There was no dust, no cobwebs; the walls and ceiling were painted bright, clean white. The light bulb in the center of the ceiling was uncovered, unadorned.

Next to the cot, on the floor, was a plainly framed photograph of Uncle Martin and Jack's father. In it, Uncle Martin looked to be twelve or thirteen, which would have made his father seven. A lock of blond-brown hair fell across his father's brow, just like it did on his; his father had the same type of Huckleberry Finn grin. The two of them held fishing poles standing next to them, and both their chests were thrust out at the camera. Uncle Martin held a string of perch out proudly. The two boys had their arms around one another's shoulders.

Someone had scribbled in blue ink at the bottom of the picture: *Jerry and Marty, buddies.* The word "buddies" had been underlined.

As he put the picture down he heard his uncle's truck returning.

He ran from the room. One of the straps ripped on his backpack. He grasped the burlap sack by the top and ran to the front door. His uncle's truck had not appeared in the circular drive yet, but he could hear it approaching.

He ran to the edge of the deck, jumped off and ran west into the woods.

In five minutes he had reached the nearest trout stream. The day was warm and he had sweated through his shirt. He kneeled and washed his face.

He took off his boots, rolled up his pants.

He waded downstream, keeping to the middle of the water. After a hundred yards he climbed out and made his presence as conspicuous as possible. He went fifty yards into the woods until he reached another, smaller stream, stepped into the middle of it, then carefully retraced his path to the larger creek.

He waded back into it and went upstream, passing the point he had started from. He went on like this for a quarter mile, once falling into a deep pool where the water was up to his chest. After another quarter mile he emerged on the other bank and set off west into the trees.

It was later in the day than he had hoped. Originally, he had planned to reach the nearest house before dark. Now he would have to spend the night in the woods.

That, he knew, would be when he was most vulnerable. His uncle was a good night hunter, had told him that night hunting was the best kind because the prey either thought you would not be there or was so terrified it tripped itself up.

He moved always west, gauging by the late afternoon sun. He had made a good mile when a noise caught his attention. He paused. He was breathing heavily; the single strap on his pack was beginning to dig into his shoulder. He took it off. Noise again. The slam of a door. It did not repeat.

He moved on. He craved sound now, thus to gauge his uncle's pursuit, but the afternoon was so still that fear invaded him for the first time. The knowledge that night was not far off didn't help. He had never spent a night alone in the woods.

He stopped, hearing a final loud noise in the distance—the angry dull boom of a shotgun?—and, stifling a stab of cold terror, he stumbled on.

Night dropped around him. One moment he could clearly distinguish the outline of trees surrounding him; the next he was effectively blind. The afternoon had darkened by degrees, and his eyes had adapted to it, but now real night had come and darkness was real and complete.

He halted. He heard his own breathing, heard the crack of dead twigs under his feet, heard little else but crickets and, far off, the questioning hoot of a waking owl.

He took a half-bag of crackers and a stale doughnut from his pack and ate, crouched at the roots of an old oak. It was getting cold. The thin windbreaker that had been more than adequate when the sun had filtered warmly through the trees now helped little, and he soon began to shiver.

"Shit," he said, hugging himself, angry at his bad planning and worse luck; "shit!"

Above his whispered exclamation of self-pity, he heard another sound.

Instinctively, a line of fear drew down his back. He had learned certain sounds in the woods. This wasn't the scratch of a squirrel, or the jumpier antics of a chipmunk. It wasn't the darting sweep of a fruit bat. It was something else.

He rose slowly, half-paralyzed by fear, his back pressed tight against the rough bark of the tree.

In front of him, something hissed and moved across his thin line of vision.

It stopped, showing itself off. It knew that it had him, and, like all cats, it almost preferred play to killing. Its eyes were like two gleaming pumpkin cutout slits, glowing. Almost by their light, he could see the prominently whiskered outline of the rest of its small face. It bared its teeth once at him, giving a short testy snarl, and then circled back on itself, into the surrounding blackness and then out of it again.

Cougar.

His uncle had told him about cougars. They hunted only at night; could drag a 900-pound moose over snow by the neck; could jump up fifteen feet with ease and cover twenty miles in one night. A man against a cougar without at least a shotgun and lots of space to fire it was a dead man. His uncle said he had once seen a man brought out of the woods who'd inadvertently cornered a female. The left side of his body was raked as if a machine had gone through it, razoring through clothes, skin, muscle, even bone. Some of the gashes had been nearly an inch deep.

This looked like that kind of cougar.

The thing slid across his line of sight, growling to itself, then turned into the darkness again. Jack heard its faint, leisurely pad, heard it suddenly stop.

The woods waited.

Out there, he felt it tense into the projectile that would fire at him out of the night, knifing into his flesh and making it night forever for him.

It pulled tighter, tighter, ready to discharge—

"Don't move, Jerry." His uncle's voice sounded calmly to his left.

The cougar sprang.

The dark exploded with light and thunder. The cougar's hissing thin face, whiskers spread over its long teeth like twin brushes, disintegrated like a crushed melon at his feet.

"Jerry—" his uncle began.

Jack peeled away from the tree trunk and ran off. His hands were his eyes; he patted them out in front of him, warding away the night and the thicket of trees. He ran into a tangle of underbrush, and his foot was grabbed by a root. He twisted to one side and fell. He pulled free, gasping, and one boot came away. He stood and stumbled on.

The night lit up ghostly in front of him. Looking up, he was dazzled by the risen, gibbous moon sliding out from behind a bank of clouds. He was in a small clearing, with a stretch of woods in front of him.

He hobbled into it.

There was enough moonlight strobing the trees ahead for him to see where he was going.

Behind and to his left, he glimpsed his uncle just descending from the clearing into the wood he inhabited.

He hobbled faster.

He cut to the right, off into a thicket away from his uncle. His feet tangled, tumbling him to the ground. He rose, catching sight of his uncle gliding like a spirit after him.

"Jerry," his uncle called out patiently.

Jack's lungs burned with insufficient oxygen. He ignored the fire, stumbling on. The moon brightened; then was lost to a cloud. Jack tripped again, and suddenly before him was the broad trunk of an old maple. He cried out but his hands did not rise fast enough as the moon returned and he saw his uncle's face beside him as the tree punched him—

He awoke in his bed, in daylight. The light was off, making the room nearly dark, but the door was open and the long windows downstairs filled the doorway with sunlight.

His uncle sat at the foot of the bed, in the dimness, staring at him. His face was blackened with cork, a camouflage cap was pulled low over his brow. Only the whites of his eyes stood out madly from his face.

His uncle spoke quietly, in horrible contrast to his appearance. "I want to tell you something, Jerry," he said. "I heard a copter this morning. It won't be long before they find you. Before they do, I have to tell you something."

Tear tracks intersected the cork markings on his face.

"I could have gone longer," he said. "I want you to know I could have gone as long as I had to. I have the will, Jerry. I've had it for a long time. I wanted to prove that to you."

Uncle Martin sat rigid and military as stone, a weeping statue. "That first time was the only time, Jerry. It never happened again. *Never.* It never happened in the Army, or the Green Berets, not anywhere. I saw what I was, and I beat it, Jerry." He sobbed, a tight gulping sound. *"I beat it."*

His uncle rose and stood stiffly beside the bed. His hands were straight at his sides, like dead things. He stared down at them. "I don't know why I touched you that time, Jerry. You meant more to me than anyone in the world. You still do. If I had known that touching you would make you act like that, I would not have done it. But I *loved* you, Jerry. And I had such feelings . . . such strong feelings, that I thought it was right to do what I did."

A great sob sought release, but his uncle held it back.

"I didn't know it was *wrong.* I learned it, though. That's what I want you to know. I learned, and it never happened again. All the time I was in the Army, and all the men and boys I saw, the feelings that went on inside me, I never let them out."

His uncle turned and looked at him earnestly. *"I had to prove it to you.* To make it right between us." Tears rolled down his face. *"You were my little brother, Jerry! You were all I had in the world!* What you did to me, the way you shut me out, it nearly *killed* me. God, I was only *fifteen,* Jerry. If only I could take that one time back . . ."

His uncle sat stiffly down on the bed, wiping a hand across his face.

"So I thought I could make it like it was again, show you that what I did meant nothing. I wanted to take it back.

"And now I have. *Oh, God, please, Jerry, tell me it never happened . . .*"

His uncle wept into his hands.

When the state troopers came through the door a half hour later, he hadn't moved. As they pulled Uncle Martin from the bed he saw his pleading eyes and he said quietly, "It never happened," and his uncle's last look was one of deliverance and peace . . .

"That's my most painful memory," he whispered to Rebecca Meyer. Somewhere he had begun to cry, and he let her hold him, rocking the poison out of him. "Oh, God," he wept, "he never touched me, Uncle Martin never touched me, *oh, Dad* . . ."

The night continued. She rocked him, and, sometime near dawn, she whispered to him, "You're well."

He laughed and said, "You're right."

He moved against her, and for a time they didn't talk. Paine fleetingly thought of the sounds of the tape in Barker's office.

"What about Gerald?" he whispered.

"Gerald can go to hell."

When they had finished, the sun was rising and she said, "What are you going to do today?"

"That depends on whether it means anything to you that I don't work for the Barker Agency anymore, and don't have a contract to find out who killed your father."

"My sister can go to hell, too," she said. She looked deep into his eyes. "Here's a contract of your own," she whispered, kissing him.

He smiled. "Then I'm going to see someone who knows more than he told me."

He tried to hold her but she got up. "I have to go. Call me later."

"I will," he said.

"Call me," she whispered to him, and suddenly sleep overtook him, and her face stayed with him, and, for a time in his sleep, he knew who she was.

T·W·E·N·T·Y O·N·E

I n the morning he felt whole. He awoke alone, but for the first time in two days he felt like a live man. His ribs ached, but it was a dull, inconsequential hurt he could live with.

He dressed and went out of the bedroom, down the long stairs and out through the front door as Gerald, in his tennis togs, came in.

"Well, well," Gerald said. "Look who's returned from the dead." His voice was mock sweet. He pointed with his racket to the far end of the driveway. "Rebecca had your car brought up here from . . . wherever it was."

He turned to go but Paine stopped him.

"Why do you hang around here?" Paine asked him.

"Two reasons," Gerald answered. "Money, and money."

"Cute answer," Paine said. "Does Rebecca know anything about your coke habit? You're pretty stupid to leave the stuff in the bathroom upstairs. I found it next to your cheap aftershave."

Gerald's face clouded. "She doesn't know about it."

Paine nodded. "I didn't think so. I've got a friend in the police department who grew up Irish poor and loves to bust rich jerks like you. Should I give him a call or would you like to get lost?"

He watched Gerald's face as the options dropped away from him.

"I'll leave," he said finally.

"Don't look so sad," Paine said. "There are plenty of other tennis courts in Westchester."

The keys were in the ignition of Paine's car. He pulled out of the driveway, feeling like he'd been away from the world for a year. His ribs were telling him that a year off might not be a bad idea.

He drove down to Croton. The blue Chrysler was gone from the front of Hartman's house. In its place was a white Merccdcs. It looked like the car that had followed him to the funeral home.

Paine went to the front door, tried the lock, which was engaged.

He stepped off the stoop and walked to the small bay window fronting the living room. He heard a television set, a baseball announcer laughing, the rise of the crowd noise and the announcer's laughter turning to excitement.

"Holy cow!" the television said. It sounded like a Yankee had hit a home run.

"Holy cow," Paine muttered to himself, shaking his head at the bad luck of the man sitting in Hartman's chair smoking a cigarette and watching the baseball game. It had to be Childs. It would be his bad luck to lose his teeth before Hartman did.

Paine walked calmly back to the front door and kicked it in with the flat of his right foot. The bolt splintered out of the jam and Paine pushed the door the rest of the way open. He walked in. Childs was up, his cigarette still in his hand.

"Shit," he said, dropping the cigarette and running to the back of the house.

Paine went after him. He kicked the television off its stand as he went by. The sound stayed on, increasing in volume. "Holy cow!" the announcer shouted.

Childs turned from the kitchen table, leveling a .44 at Paine as he entered. It was a wide miss. Paine ran at him and drove him into the refrigerator. Childs dropped the gun and tried to drive his fist into the back of Paine's head. He struck at Paine's rib cage. Paine groaned and loosened his grip. Childs scrambled away. Paine straightened to see the back door fly back on its hinges. Childs disappeared into the backyard.

Paine followed. His hurt lope turned into angry pursuit. Childs vanished into the yawning opening of the garage. Paine saw another figure in there, working under the upraised hood of the blue Chrysler.

Paine returned to the kitchen, retrieved Childs's .44 and walked back into the yard, keeping the wide mouth of the garage diagonal to him.

"Let's talk," Paine called into the garage.

"Fuck you," Hartman's voice answered.

The blue Chrysler's rear end butted invitingly out the garage door. Paine took aim at it, putting a slug into the rear panel just above the gas tank.

"Shit," Childs shouted from the far reaches of the garage.

"Here's what's going to happen," Paine said. "I'm going to pump shots into the gas tank until one of them hits it.

When that happens, gasoline and metal will blow right through your fucking faces. Got anything to say?"

"Fuck you," Hartman called out.

Paine put another slug into the side of the car, a little lower.

"Maybe the next one," Paine said.

"Jesus," Childs answered, but once again Hartman yelled, "Fuck you!"

Paine aimed another shot at the Chrysler, shattering the back windshield.

There was fast arguing and Paine moved toward the side of the garage as Hartman ran out into the open with a shotgun, pulling off one chamber and shouting. He stopped shouting and found himself out in the open with Paine behind him. Paine took careful aim. *"Drop it,"* he said, but Hartman wheeled with the shotgun, pulling off the other chamber. His shot flew into the air as Paine's hit him just under the chin and he got a surprised look on his face and took a couple of breaths through the hole in his neck and then dropped, gasping on the ground like a banked catfish.

"Enough of this shit," Paine said. He walked to the doorway of the garage and fired two more shots into the tank of the Chrysler.

One of them flared the tank and Childs ran screaming out of the garage as it blew. The back of his shirt caught fire. He ran blindly at Paine, and Paine punched him and threw him onto his back and snuffed the flames from his shirt.

Paine stood and put his foot on Childs's chest.

"Let's talk."

"We should have killed you in that parking lot," Childs whimpered.

"You were supposed to, asshole, weren't you?" Paine moved his foot up to Childs's neck and pressed.

Childs said nothing, so Paine pressed harder. "Weren't you?"

"Yes," Childs gasped.

"Who do you work for? Hartman told me you worked for Paterna but that was bullshit, right?"

Childs said nothing, and Paine increased the pressure on his neck until he began to fight for breath.

"Tell me. That's Paterna's Mercedes out front. Who gave it to you?"

Childs was losing his battle for breath; he nodded abruptly, and when Paine released the pressure on his windpipe he gasped, "Henry Kopiak."

"You work for Kopiak? Paterna did, too?"

Childs nodded listlessly.

From inside, the baseball game still droned on loudly, balls and strikes, runs and outs, the passing of an early autumn afternoon with a summer game.

Paine bent down over Childs, the twinge of his broken ribs telling him he shouldn't do that. "Call an ambulance for your asshole friend," he said. "And like I told him, you're the kind of scumbags that'll never get it right."

T·W·E·N·T·Y T·W·O

Rebecca answered, and he said, "Hello."

"Jack," she said.

"You sound relieved to hear from me."

"Someone threatened to kill me this morning."

There was a cold place in his heart. "Do you know who it was?"

She sounded upset. "No."

"I don't want you to stay there," Paine said. "There's a place upstate my brother and I own." He told her about the key in the hollowed stump. "Go there and wait for me. I think I'm at the end of this thing."

"Where are you, Jack?"

"I'm going to see your father's lawyer, Henry Kopiak. He was the one who pulled Paterna's strings. When I'm finished with him I'll meet you. Would you rather I call Bob Petty?"

"I don't trust anyone."

"Then do what I said. Someone is getting very desperate, Rebecca."

"I love you," she said.

She hung up before he did.

There was nothing phony about Henry Kopiak's office. It was the real thing, not like Les Paterna's cobbled dream of class. This was the Princeton Club, the good old men, the yachts and polo ponies, the Governor's Ball, the handshakes in small sitting rooms after brandy and cigars. Old money. The root within the root of all evil.

When he walked in, Kopiak was staring out a wide window that gave the same view of the Hudson that Morris Grumbach had bought for himself. His hands were behind his back, the classic pose of rich lawyers in deep thought.

"I wasn't able to find Paterna's brown folder before I got fired," Paine said.

"That doesn't matter," Kopiak said, not turning. "Gloria Fulman and I wanted to see how much you knew. It was Gloria who decided to have you discredited and then killed. There was also the slim chance that you would find the folder, which would tell us who was killing everyone."

Kopiak turned. On the low sill of the wide window was a bottle of Chivas Regal and a single crystal glass.

"I don't want to die, Mr. Paine," Kopiak said. "It's as simple as that. I've tried to control this thing all along, but someone has been killing everyone down the line and I know that I'm at the top of the list. Gloria Fulman is already a virtual prisoner in her Boston apartments; there was an attempt on her life when she was in New York and I just can't live like that. I'd rather go to prison than be dead."

Kopiak's hands shook. Paine had seen him that one time in his office, and now his clubbiness and arrogance had faded like an outmatched number 10 horse in a crowded field. He was a frightened, beaten man.

"I've telephoned the one other person left in this thing, and when he gets here I intend to settle with him and then turn myself in." He smiled wanly at Paine. "You may do the honors, if you wish."

"I'd like to hear the whole thing," Paine said.

Kopiak ran his hands through his hair. There was a photo on his desk, framed, turned so that Paine or any other visitor could see it, of a smiling, middle-aged woman flanked by two college boys. The woman looked content. The boys looked like the kind that got letters on their jackets, drank moderately, had perky girlfriends.

"I want you to know something first," Kopiak said. He managed to pour himself another drink and get half of it down. "I want you to know that I made two mistakes in my career, and I never did anything else wrong in forty-five years of practice." His voice strengthened with self-justification. "That's a long time, Mr. Paine. Forty-five years."

He lowered his voice, using his glass as an emphatic pointer. "There was a time when I wanted to run for office, Mr. Paine. That was my weakness. To do that, you have to make connections, and you have to make money. I made both.

"I met Morris Grumbach and his wife, Jane, at a fund-raising dinner for a local congressman. I was up on the same slate for state senator. In those days I was surrounded by men who thought I could go far beyond that. Congressman, they said, and then senator, and then . . ." He laughed bitterly. "Those were the Kennedy years, and a Catholic Pollack with connections could dream.

"Grumbach was a blowhard, but not unpleasant. Came into his money almost by mistake; his father had filed a basic patent and the family got rich overnight. He acted like he still didn't know if he deserved it.

"But Jane believed he deserved it, all right. And more. She had been born for that money, and she acted like it had always belonged to her. She thought she was royalty and acted like it.

"I didn't see all this at first, of course. But that night she seemed to take an inordinate interest in me. Fawned over me, almost. I was flattered, and, I think, my wife was a little jealous. It turned out Jane wanted something from me. She never hesitated in going after something she wanted.

"She pledged a lot of money to my campaign. As I say, I was flattered. And I needed the money. But the next week she came to my office and we had a little private talk. She had already checked me out, long before that fund-raiser, but I didn't know that then. There was something I'd done for my father-in-law, just after passing the bar, and I didn't think a soul on earth knew about it. But she did. She was very discreet about it, very gentle, but also very clear."

Kopiak looked down at the thin pool of scotch in his glass and emptied it. He went to the windowsill and poured another drink, setting it down on the ledge and staring at it. He looked around at Paine.

"She had me by the balls. With her contribution, which I had already spent, I had enough money for my campaign to really get off the ground. My practice was doing well also. My first son had just been born, giving me a real family for the first time in my life. With one phone call she could end it all." He fingered the glass on the ledge. "Or, she hinted, she could take out her checkbook and write another check."

He picked up the glass and moved it to the desk, sitting down in his chair. "She wrote another check. While she did that she told me what she wanted.

"It didn't seem like much, the way she told it. She had a way of talking that made you think you had nothing to do with her business, that she was merely hiring you for the details she couldn't handle herself. It was her way of making you feel as if you weren't in any way responsible. Which wasn't true, of course."

Kopiak held out a shaking hand to Paine. "I believe you have two packets of photographs?"

Paine took them out and handed them over. Kopiak took the pictures of Les Paterna, Lucas Druckman and Jeffrey Steppen and put them to one side. He spread out the other three and stared at them, as if coming across an old memory in a scrapbook, something momentous, perhaps, and, though buried by time, finding a host of dredged and still-sharp memories surface. His hand moved to his drink and, without removing his eyes from the three photos, he brought his scotch to his lips and drank. When the glass was empty he set it down.

"These two," he said quietly, as if to himself, pointing with his forefinger to the picture of the man and woman standing next to the new car, "were Gloria's father and mother. He worked for an aviation firm in southern California. She was their only child, and they had her late in life. He died about eight years ago, a massive coronary. His wife died two months later."

He moved to the second photograph, his finger trembling slightly over the man and woman in the field with the horse in the background. "Dolores's parents. Originally from New Mexico. They moved to California in 1966. Dolores was born two years later. She was their only child. They died in an auto accident in 1975. The coroner's report said he was driving while intoxicated."

The finger moved to the third photo, the corporate head shot of the man with the wry smile. "Rebecca's father. He served in Korea in 1953, worked for a P.R. firm when this picture was taken, and, after his wife left with their other child, a son, he went back to serve in Vietnam in 1968. Suicide ran in his family. The wife and son left no tracks, and he never saw them again. After he got back from the war he hung himself in 1972."

He stared at the three photos as if waiting for them to speak. But the dead don't speak. Then, seemingly of its own accord, his hand moved to the other three photographs, coming down flat on all of them.

"And this," he said, "was the man who stole the three girls away from their real parents."

Kopiak reached back toward the windowsill for the scotch bottle, but instead of taking it he knocked it to the rug. The sweet-sour smell of spilled Chivas filled the office.

"Oh, Jesus," he sobbed in self-pity, putting his head in his hands. He looked up into Paine's face, searching it for something he didn't find.

He ran his hand once more through his hair and continued. "Jane Grumbach was from an underworld family in California. Morris had nothing to do with the Mafia, but he fell in love with her and she ran him like a puppet. She was a very strong woman. Marrying Morris made her legitimate rich, but she never forgot how she'd grown up. She got whatever she wanted. And she wanted little girls. She couldn't have them herself, and adoption was long and would not give her exactly what she required, so she hired Jeffrey Steppen to get them for her. She heard about Steppen through her family; he had been kicked out of the FBI but knew everything about getting things like phony birth records and Social Security numbers. It was easy for her to buy Steppen; she had enough to blackmail him to begin with through her underworld acquaintances, and he was a sucker for money and the trappings of it. He gave her some trouble later, when his side businesses kept getting him into hot water with various mob people, but he was valuable enough to her that she put up with his face changes and she always paid his bills when it was necessary. She even made Morris work with him and set up Bravura Enterprises after he became Les Paterna.

"Steppen found a couple of Hollywood leeches named Izzy and Mona to do the actual snatchings. He had pictures taken of various children that fitted the description of what Jane Grumbach wanted, and then she picked the photos of the babies she wanted and Izzy and Mona stole them. She wanted three daughters, and she got them, in 1962, 1965 and 1968."

Kopiak looked around for his scotch bottle, located it on the floor and picked it up. There was enough unspilled Chivas in the bottle for a two-finger drink. "And I did the paperwork. Steppen provided the documents, I did the rest. I knew the right people, Jane Grumbach knew anyone I didn't, and the job got done." He drank the last of the scotch. "I didn't win my election that first year I met the Grumbachs, but my law practice thrived. I became the Grumbach family's lawyer. I watched the three girls grow up. I went to their high school graduations." He put the empty crystal glass down, next to the picture of his wife and sons. He looked at it wistfully. "I sent them presents each Christmas."

"Did the girls know about it?" Paine asked.

"No," Kopiak said dreamily. "Not until just before their mother died, about a year ago. Rebecca found these pictures of yours and confronted her father; he was drunk and feeling guilty and he told her everything. Her mother just laughed, told them they were better off and that she'd done them a favor. It must have been terrible for them . . ."

"Who killed everyone, Kopiak?"

Kopiak stood. "I don't know . . ." he said. He paced to the window, turned his back and assumed the position Paine had seen him in when he came in. He stared down through the glass into nothing, into the river, perhaps.

Suddenly he seemed to peer closely at something, and his body tightened and he said, as if in revelation, "Oh—"

Paine heard the shot. The window had a two-foot hole in it where Kopiak's face had been. Imploded fragments of blood-tinted glass showered the room.

Paine crouched his way to the corner of the window, stepping over Kopiak's nearly beheaded body, and glanced cautiously outside. He saw nothing: street, low buildings, river. Keeping low, he ran for the door of the office and down to the street. He still saw nothing.

As he got into his car and headed north a tan Ford immediately settled in behind him. Paine drove a couple of blocks and the Ford kept its distance. When Paine next glanced in his rearview mirror the driver of the tan Ford had put a red flasher on the roof and a siren began to wail.

"Shit," Paine said.

He came to a stop at the curb and the tan Ford pulled in behind him. Paine watched in the rearview mirror as the driver got out, keeping his head down. It looked like he was studying his ticket book.

Paine glanced away and when he looked back the driver was not there anymore.

"Move over, asshole."

The driver was behind him, and Paine saw the .38 before he heard the voice. The voice was Dannon's. Dannon opened the back door of Paine's car and slid across the seat.

"Drive," he said.

The round cool mouth of the .38 kissed the back of Paine's neck.

"Where do you want me to go?"

"The old beat, Jackie-boy."

Paine drove slowly. He took each turn cautiously, keeping his hands in view on the wheel.

"Did Jane Grumbach own you long?" Paine asked.

The mouth of the .38 bumped his neck as Dannon laughed. "I don't know what you're talking about, fuckhead."

"The way I figure it, you took care of the local police for Kopiak and the Grumbachs. The thing I can't figure out is why you killed Kopiak and the rest—why derail the gravy train?"

"Kopiak is dead?"

"His brains are all over his office."

"I was on the way to his office when I saw you. I didn't kill anybody," Dannon said angrily, jamming the gun into Paine's neck.

"Did—"

"Just drive," Dannon snapped.

"Any special place you want me to go?"

"You know where." Paine's hands tightened on the wheel. In the back seat, Dannon was solemn. After a moment he asked, "Kopiak's really dead?"

"Yes."

"Drive," he repeated.

Paine drove.

When they got to the end of the street by the railroad station, Dannon told him to slow down. "You know where to park," he said. Paine pulled the car over to the curb in front of the bench where he'd found the man with the wedge out of his neck. That had been night, and this was day, but the sky was gunmetal gray and the buildings were high and blocked the sun. It might as well be night.

"Get out of the car."

Paine got out. The day became night for him, and the other, earlier night began to unreel in his head like a spool of shadowy movie film. He saw the man with the wedge out of his neck on the ground, face down; he heard Dannon's running footsteps ahead of him, saw the man in the leather jacket running, saw the two of them turn a corner and disappear.

"Walk."

Paine walked. He followed each invisible step as he had then. Dannon's .38 was in his back but he didn't feel it. In his mind he was running, in his mind he went to the corner, stopped, listened in the night for the sound of running men.

"Keep moving, asshole."

In his head, he heard Dannon shout for him, turned, saw movement in the alley, followed . . .

"That's the way, asshole, I see you remember."

Paine's mind fogged. The movie film unreeled. There was a groaning, thick ache in his stomach. He couldn't see clearly. He heard movement behind him. Dannon. Ahead, under the sloping high sides of apartment buildings, the spiderworks of rusting fire escapes, the tattered flags of wet wash and, up high, the twisted praying metal hands of television antennae, under all this, in the dim walkway scattered with a maze of cartons, broken furniture, the broken innards of a television separated from its praying hands above, he saw movement—*the boy in the leather jacket?*—saw a figure step out of the deep dream of the night and point something at him . . .

"Paaaaaaaaaine!"

He remembered, but it was no better; the night was the same, his mind a foggy mess, his arm raised next to him, feeling like it didn't belong to him, like his finger had that night when Ginny walked in on him with that bullet in the chamber of his .38 staring at him, his finger becoming apart from him, thinking for him, and the night became bright with light and the figure in the leather jacket became one with the ground and the flash from the thing the boy pointed at him did not go out like the blinding flash he saw next to him—

"I have a present for you, Paine."

The film spooled onto the ground, the movie was over and he still didn't understand the ending.

Dannon stepped back away from Paine. "I'm going to give you a present before I blow your fucking head apart."

He brought his gun to eye level, sighting along the barrel at Paine's face. "The way I see it, you killed Kopiak and the rest of them. At least, for my purposes you did. And the way I see it I had to shoot you during apprehension. But before I do that I'm going to tell you what happened that night. You didn't kill that kid. I did. The little fucker was running numbers for me, and he'd started skimming. The guy with the briefcase was another of my problems. So were you. So I decided to get rid of all my problems at once.

"I drugged you that night, asshole. Just enough to make you punchy without putting you out. I set up a meeting between the briefcase man and the little shit, and told the bastard that if he took care of briefcase he'd be even with me. Then I told him to wait for me in this alley with a flashlight. Then I called you in. You would have seen Martians if I'd told you to. I told the kid to turn on the flashlight, slipped your .38 out and did him, then put the .38 into your hand. It was easy."

Dannon took careful aim along the barrel of his gun. He

moved it up a fraction of an inch, to the center of Paine's temple.

"Nice clean shot for my old partner." He smiled. "Turns out you weren't a bad cop after all. So long, fuckhead."

Paine heard a shot, but it didn't come from Dannon's .38. Dannon gave a short cry of surprise and fell forward. Two more shots went into his prone body, making it jump lifelessly.

Paine ran to the mouth of the alley but the car had gunned its engine and was gone. He crossed the street. There, a car's width out from the curb, were three .30-06 shells, their caliber neatly stamped in a circlet on the back. He picked them up. Near them was a small white rectangle with the name "Johnson" written on it. When he turned the rectangle over, it became a photograph, a corporate head shot of a man with a wry smile who had committed suicide in 1972.

Paine pulled out the worn envelopes of photos in his pocket, saw the name "Mr. Johnson" written on them in Morris Grumbach's arrogant scrawl and Dolores Grumbach's careful script.

The world upended.

For a moment Paine didn't breathe. He saw her face in front of him, felt the essence of her that had danced out of his reach since his eyes had first found hers and sought the answer to the mystery there.

He knew the answer now, why she had affected him so deeply.

She was his mirror image.

And he knew what she was going to do.

Running for his car, Paine said, "Jesus."

T·W·E·N·T·Y T·H·R·E·E

Venus and Mars.

Paine's hands were cold on the steering wheel. His mind was cold in his head. Through the window, as he passed the bridge down to his left and the lights of the city began to fade to memory behind him, he saw the stars and the two planets emerge. Mars and Venus. They were farther apart now, the conjunction passing, and they whirled off into space away from one another, two entities that never had belonged together. They were literally on the opposite sides of the earth, Venus close to the sun, Mars out past our planet in the colder reaches of the solar system, away from the sun's heat, and there was nothing that man could do to change that. Venus was love, Mars was war, and man couldn't change that, either.

He drove. He passed the spot where the motorist had

been pulled over that night, when the red and white of the state trooper's flasher had reminded him of Mars and Venus. The spot on the roadside was empty now, empty as space above. He drove on. Too late for after-work drinkers tonight. Too late for everybody.

When he was nearly there he knew that he could not catch her. She would drive as fast as she had to, and even though there was only a matter of minutes between them, it might as well be eternity.

Above, through the windshield, Venus was pushed below the horizon, leaving Mars to stare at him like an evil eye.

He pulled off the highway. There was a gas station and it was closed, and then there was a country store with an outside phone but the receiver was dead. And then there was a bar and the music was loud from the jukebox, and an early drunk was telling his friend about the bass he caught—but there was a phone and he put change into it and there was ringing and ringing and then she picked it up.

"I found the key, Jack," she said tonelessly. "In the hollowed trunk like you said."

He knew her voice; it was his own voice in the times when the numbness had taken him over. It was not calm; it was beyond that in a place where there was a clarity that was pure and absolute.

"Rebecca, listen to me—"

"I'm going to kill myself, Jack. You know that. This is the way it had to be all along and you can't stop me from doing it. Dannon was the last. Will you listen to me, Jack? I love you, please listen to me."

"Oh, God, Rebecca—"

"Listen to me, Jack."

Her voice was like his finger had been when it was on the trigger of his .38, when it had *become* him, and if he did not listen to her she would hang up and he would lose her then and there.

"Yes," he said.

"In the beginning, when I found out who I really am, I used to think a lot about being a Grumbach. And I knew in my heart that I would have been a different person if my real father had raised me. I know there are some things that would have been the same no matter what, but I was sure that there were a lot of things that were put into me by the Grumbachs, things that made me what I am, that would have been different.

"That was the worst thing. Realizing that they had robbed me of who I was supposed to be. And all because the woman who I had known as my mother had decided that she wanted three little girls and that no one was going to stop her from having them.

"My father felt guilty about what my mother had done, but it didn't seem to matter to him whether we were there or not. But my mother wanted us, and we became what she wanted us to be. Gloria was the worst; when she found out who she really was she agreed with my mother that she was lucky. That made my mother very proud.

"I killed my mother. She was drinking one night and I broke apart two dozen sleeping pills and mixed a good bit of the powder in with each of her scotches. Dolores knew about it but said nothing; she said she would help me kill my father but she couldn't and then when I did she couldn't handle it and she killed herself."

There was silence; the faint whistle of electricity running through wires.

"When I murdered my father I took one of his guns, and I made him go to that hotel with me. I made him stand on a chair and tie the rope to the ceiling, and then make a noose at the other end and put it around his neck. He didn't think

I was going to kill him. He thought it was some kind of game; he kept saying, 'Whatever the problem is, I'll give you the money for it.' I made him address the envelope to be left at the Mallard, and then call you. I told him what to say. When he got to the part about hanging himself I kicked the chair out from under him."

Her voice was tired, distant, little above the faint whistle of electricity. "I wanted to make them all hang themselves, but it just didn't work out that way."

She stopped speaking, and for a moment Paine thought she was gone. He put more change into the telephone, and was about to call her name when she spoke again. She sounded very far away from him, on Mars.

"I used you, Jack. I couldn't get beyond Paterna by myself and I needed someone to find out who the rest of them were. I'm sorry I did that. I fell in love with you very quickly.

"I want you to remember that, Jack. I love you. If none of this had happened, I could have loved you for a long time. If there's anywhere after this, I still will."

She was beyond Mars, in the cold reaches of space. "Don't try to follow me. I know you as well as you know yourself, because in many ways we're the same, and I know that you don't have it in you to do what I'm going to do. You're too good for that. You might go to the edge, and peer over, but something will always hold you and keep you from falling. When you find me tonight you might want to follow, and you might think you can, but you can't. Maybe you'll think of me as holding you from now on."

Her voice became even farther away, dreamy. "There's something for you at the Mallard Hotel, Jack. It's addressed to Mr. Johnson. Please tell me you'll take care of it. It will end all this forever."

From her voice, he knew the moment was coming. "Rebecca—"

"Promise me, Jack."

"*Oh, God, I promise. Rebecca*—"

"I'm going to hang myself, Jack."

He screamed into the phone but he heard the receiver drop and heard her cry out, a muffled "Oh" that sounded almost like release.

Outside, the night was silent and cold as death. Overhead, Mars was gone now, too, eaten by the horizon, but there were stars like spread gems, blue, yellow and white, and there, just overhead, the thumb-smudge of the Hercules cluster, M13, that he had looked at with Tom what seemed like a universe ago.

The constellation Gemini was pushing its autumn stars up overhead. Gemini—the mythological twins Castor and Pollux, only one of whom was immortal. Castor and Pollux, special protectors of warriors.

In the sky, Gemini wheeled north.

Paine followed.

T·W·E·N·T·Y F·O·U·R

C old night.

The gun, the bottle.

For Paine, this time, there was no third choice. No A.A. meetings, no sincere bullshit, no upbeat slogans about "learning to like yourself." No suicide-prevention hot line this time, no cool, calm voices coming out of the phone, trying to climb into the dark crawlspace in his head ("Where are you? What are you doing now? When did you start to feel like this?").

Tonight it was the gun, the bottle.

Hartman's .44 lay on the ground next to him. He sat with his back against the observatory, staring up into a sky that might as well be empty of stars. The telescope was blind, its dome sealed against the intrusion of starlight. Above, the stars of Hercules and Gemini dominated the sky, but Paine was as blind to their inevitable passage as the telescope.

Next to the .44 was the long, square bottle of Jim Beam

he had bought in the bar. The bartender had given him an odd look, but the twenty-dollar bill Paine had given him made the odd look disappear. Paine had almost forgotten what a bar smelled like; the distinctive, hidden-alcohol smell. All those bottles side by side, snugly shelved up to the ceiling, enough to make a man drunk for a month or two—all the *weight* of that potential bender seeping through the bottle glass into the dry close air. The Jim Beam's white plastic twist cap was marred where his fingers had worried it open and closed. He had fought the idea of starting immediately, outside the bar, emptying the bourbon into his stomach and mind, not even waiting to get up north.

He stared at the bottle of bourbon. *This is why we are called thinking beings,* he thought. An animal would have used the gun or the bourbon by now, and thus made room on the planet for more, better animals. But not man. To the end he was an animal with a plan. He would argue with himself constantly, think about the things that had happened to him, try to feel sorry for himself and the others he had dragged through his life even as he had been dragged through it himself. Man, it seemed, always manufactured choices for himself.

The gun, the bottle.

The gun . . .

He remembered the first time he had picked up a gun. His father had been cleaning it in his study, and then the phone rang and he had gone to answer it in the hallway. Paine had come running in with his baseball glove to ask if he could go to the ball field with his friends. He saw the door to the study open, heard his father on the phone down the hall. He went into the study, saw the gun lying there, blue chrome steel, a handle like polished mahogany. It looked like a sophisticated toy. The cleaning materials were still laid out around it, but the gun was whole. He picked it up.

It was heavier than he thought it would be. He hefted it in his palm, then closed his hands around the stock, turning it toward the wall and aiming it like Elliot Ness rubbing out the Chicago mob—"Pow!"—then turning it to look down the barrel, his thumb slipping as he turned to see his father there in the doorway, as the gun slipped and he squeezed his grip to keep it from falling, his thumb tightening on the trigger.

The gun said *click* and his father hit him for the first and only time, his open palm across the back of Jack's head as he shouted, "My *God!*" as much at himself as at his son.

The bottle . . .

The bottle was harder to remember, because it had come on slowly. Beers in high school, gradually bourbon in the Army and then both after work with Bob Petty, searching harder as time went on for the place that made him numb, the place where all the bad places didn't go away but at least had a hard time making it clearly through his head . . .

The gun, the bottle.

Both.

Neither . . .

Rebecca Meyer's face pushed into his mind. He remembered the hours before sunrise, the dark outline of her sleeping profile. He thought of the swimming seas of her eyes that had trapped and pulled him down into their depths. He wanted to swim there now again.

He looked toward the house, saw the bright light in the window, thought of the empty sea of Rebecca that was left in there.

Emptiness settled into him again. He looked down at the bourbon, remembered the dry, oppressive odor of the bar.

The bottle.

The gun.

He picked up the .44, pressed the cold heaviness of the barrel against his temple. He felt his being flowing into his finger. He was drained, an empty thing, and only his finger was alive. He felt his finger on the trigger, felt himself, the trigger, pulling, pulling—

He brought the .44 down hard, smashing it into the bottle of Jim Beam. The bottle broke, sour bourbon splashing out of it and soaking into the thirsty ground. Paine trembled, his arm rigid, the hand holding the .44 jamming it into the broken bottle. He felt the sharp bright sting of a glass cut on his finger, felt the sensation of it blossom from his finger up through his hand and arm and into his head.

He saw her face again, heard her telling him what he knew in his heart and mind to be true.

"You're right, Rebecca, I can't."

His hand relaxed, letting the .44 go, letting it wash itself in a sea of spent bourbon.

He looked up and saw the stars.

He sat for a long time under the stars and said good-bye to her.

Then he got up and went to keep his promise.

T·W·E·N·T·Y F·I·V·E

No smiles at the front door this time.

Paine managed his way past the first guard, but the desk man in the lobby was the real general. Paine couldn't even see the private elevator from the partitioned area around the man's desk; for all he knew the slim golden door was a wonderland illusion.

"Tell her it's about her daughter," Paine said to the stone face of the desk man.

The stone face spoke into the phone, and then the stone turned to soft wax and he said to Paine, "You may go up."

Paine walked past the desk and walked to the left and found the private elevator set in the marble facade. It was just where he had left it.

The doors opened, he got in, the elevator went up and he got off. The hallway, the right turn, the huge double doors. The ex-boxer doorman with the flat eyes nodded and said his name and the double doors magically opened once more.

Gloria Fulman was waiting for him in the entrance hall. There were a lot of bags packed in the foyer. She must have worked up quite a sweat telling all those maids and doormen where to pile things up.

"Little trip?" Paine asked.

"The other room, please," she said. Paine followed.

No tea sandwiches this time, or little cups of coffee with doilies under the saucers. Gloria Fulman went to one Sheraton sofa and sat down. Paine sat on its twin, facing her, and crossed his legs. The door to the pantry was in his line of sight to the left. The hallway was slightly to his right; another door was to his extreme right, almost beyond his peripheral vision, but he thought he'd be able to handle it if anyone came through.

Paine's right hand rested lightly on the front of his jacket, near his .38.

The coffee stains had been cleaned from the Persian rug. Gloria Fulman continued to glare at him, so Paine spoke first.

"I've been wondering what kind of man your husband is. He must be a lot like Morris Grumbach. He can forget about ever running for President."

"You said something about my daughter, Mr. Paine."

He watched her. He enjoyed watching her, and there was some guilt in this but not much. He was watching her the way she had watched him, the way Barker had watched everyone in his life, the way all people with the big hand watch the loser with the pair of deuces. He watched her wheels turn; watched her go through and reject the options —money, violence, blackmail, murder—and then he saw her come to a dead stop. The wheels rusted. She knew she had lost. The bags in the hallway, she knew, would not be packed into the Rolls-Royce and driven, along with her and her infant daughter and husband, to a private plane in a far and quiet corner of Logan Airport. She would not leave the country for a place without extradition, where her money, safe and available in Switzerland, would soon make her powerful and wanted again. She would not own the colorfully corrupt mayor, the police chief and whatever ministers, civil servants, private maids and thugs she would possibly need. She knew that none of this would happen now, because she was too late.

She sat for a few moments, and Paine watched many of the fancy parts of her flake away, and when she was finished with her inventory of options and her miniature devolution she said, in a voice that was small and almost private, the voice that was deep inside her behind all the masks, in whatever tiny place she kept things that she really believed, "She's better off with me."

"I bet your mother said that each morning," Paine said.

He took a slim envelope from his jacket pocket and slid it across the coffee table at her. She looked at it but did not pick it up. Scribbled across the face of it was the name "Mr. Johnson" in Rebecca Meyer's handwriting.

"Inside the envelope is a *Los Angeles Times* clipping on your daughter's kidnapping," Paine said to her. "Rebecca found it in Les Paterna's brown folder, along with a copy of the birth certificate he falsified for you. He was probably going to use it on you somewhere down the line, when things at Bravura Enterprises got a little tight.

"I've made plenty of copies of it. A policeman friend of mine has one, and he got in touch with a man in the Boston office of the FBI who will come to chat with you after I leave. I heard this morning, before I came over here, that there's a very happy couple in Pasadena who had given up hope that their infant daughter would be found. He's a sanitation worker, and she has to work as a salesgirl in a mall part-time, but they get by. From what I hear, they miss their little girl a lot."

He got up and left. He walked to the door and let himself out into the hallway, then he let himself out the front door, leaving it open for the doorman with the flat stare and black shiny shoes. He went to the elevator and the elevator brought him down to the lobby and he walked toward the desk man.

He felt the bulge of his .38 in his jacket, and he took it out as he went by and put it gently on the desk.

Outside, the day had started cloudy, but there were some breaks in the clouds and it looked like there might be sun.